"A little comfo **S0-AVO-754** **rolled onto his back then drew her toward him until her head rested on his shoulder and his arm wrapped around her.**

She gave a quiet little laugh. "At least I'm not cold now." Unable to resist, she snuggled a little closer and inhaled his scent. Wonderful. And the way her boots were getting warmer, she figured they'd both be safe. Another couple of minutes and they'd have to back away from the fire or completely change position.

But right now she wanted to revel in the rare experience of physical closeness with another human being. With a man. Since coming home she'd avoided it, feeling that she was too messed up to get involved without hurting someone.

Yeah, she was adapting pretty well, but if her paranoia of the past few days didn't make it clear that she wasn't completely recovered, nothing would.

And if she couldn't trust her own mind and feelings, she wasn't fit to be anyone's companion.

MURDERED
IN CONARD
COUNTY

New York Times Bestselling Author
RACHEL LEE

Recycling programs
for this product may
not exist in your area.

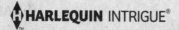

Printed in U.S.A.

Recycling programs
for this product may
not exist in your area.

978-1-335-64108-3

Murdered in Conard County

Copyright © 2019 by Susan Civil Brown

Printed in U.S.A.

Rachel Lee was hooked on writing by the age of twelve and practiced her craft as she moved from place to place all over the United States. This *New York Times* bestselling author now resides in Florida and has the joy of writing full-time.

Books by Rachel Lee

Harlequin Intrigue

Conard County: The Next Generation

Cornered in Conard County
Missing in Conard County
Murdered in Conard County

Harlequin Romantic Suspense

Conard County: The Next Generation

Guardian in Disguise
The Widow's Protector
Rancher's Deadly Risk
What She Saw
Rocky Mountain Lawman
Killer's Prey
Deadly Hunter
Snowstorm Confessions
Undercover Hunter
Playing with Fire
Conard County Witness
A Secret in Conard County
A Conard County Spy
Conard County Marine
Undercover in Conard County
Conard County Revenge
Conard County Watch

Visit the Author Profile page at Harlequin.com.

CAST OF CHARACTERS

Blaire Afton—Wyoming State park ranger and law enforcement. An army veteran with experience guarding supply convoys in Afghanistan. Some post-traumatic stress. Won't sit idly by while a murderer is being hunted.

Gus Maddox—Ranger and law officer with the US Forest Service. Also a special ops veteran, with some post-traumatic stress and a bad relationship in his past. Happiest on his horse, Scrappy. Friends with Blaire and willing to help her in her quest no matter what.

Jeff, Karl and Will—The Hunt Club. These three have been hunting buddies since childhood. One evening after a day of hunting deer, they concoct a game to stalk real human beings and plan undetectable murders. Two of them go too far and begin killing people.

Jeff Walston—Member of The Hunt Club and the weak link. He doesn't want to kill and becomes a threat to the group.

Gage Dalton—Sheriff of Conard County; a man with a history in the DEA with the scars to prove it.

Mark Jasper—Victim in Blaire's state park. Shot in the tent he was sharing with his toddler son.

Gideon Ironheart—Horse rancher and trainer who gives Blaire a horse so she and Gus can use it to track the killer.

Prologue

Three years earlier

"Have either of you ever heard of Leopold and Loeb? They thought they could commit the perfect murder."

A large fire burned in the huge stone fireplace, casting dancing tongues of orange light and inky shadows around the cabin's sitting room. The wood sizzled and crackled, adding its dry music to the light and occasionally loud pops that sounded almost like gunshots.

The log walls, burnished by the years, added weight to the entire scene. Trophy heads of bighorn sheep, elk and deer hung everywhere, beneath each a plaque memorializing a past hunter.

Clearly this was a hunting lodge, one of generous size, able to house a fairly large party. But its heyday was in the past and now only three men occupied it.

It seemed like the last place on earth three men would plot murders.

Dressed in camouflage, their orange caps and vests tossed onto a nearby chest, they sat in a semicircle of comfortable lounge chairs in front of the fire, sipping brandy from snifters. Two of them enjoyed fat cigars with a surprisingly pleasant aroma.

"It was really cold out there," remarked one of them, a man with dark hair and a luxuriant mustache who appeared to be about thirty, maybe a couple of years older. He'd been the one who had asked the question about Leopold and Loeb, but having received no response, he dropped it. For now.

"Good for the deer, Will," said the man nearest him. His name was Karl, and he looked like his Nordic ancestors, with pale hair and skin and frigid blue eyes. The deer he referred to had been field dressed and was hanging in a shed outside, protected from scavengers.

"Yeah," said Jeff, the third of them. He had the kind of good looks that could have gotten him cast on a TV drama, but he also had a kink in his spine from a military injury and he didn't quite sit or stand straight. He often endured pain but seldom showed it. "It's probably already frozen stiff."

"Like a board," Karl agreed. "Thank goodness we have a sling on our side-by-sides."

"And tomorrow maybe we'll get an elk," Jeff added. They'd won the drawing for a coveted license for an elk, and since they'd been hoping for one for years, this was no small deal.

Silence fell for a while, except for the crackling of the fire. Three men, looking very content, enjoying their hunting lodge after a successful day. Except one of them was not quite content.

Will spoke. "Do you two ever get tired of this hunting trip? Every year since we were boys, coming up here with our dads. Now just the three of us."

"Something wrong with the company?" Karl drawled.

"Of course not," Will answered. "It's just that I was thinking we've been doing this so many years, and we've never gone home empty-handed. Not much of a challenge, is it?"

Jeff nearly gaped. They'd spent the better part of three days tracking the buck that was now hanging in the shed. "We almost missed that mature eight-pointer. He was smart."

"We still got him," Will pointed out.

Karl spoke. "The elk will be even more of a challenge. What do you want, Will? To stop making these trips? I thought we were doing it more for the time away together. Three guys, brandy and cigars, traipsing around in the woods on the cusp of winter... A lot of guys would envy us."

"We aren't a lot of guys. In fact, I believe we're smarter than the average bear. All of us."

"So?"

"So, how about we hunt a different kind of prey? Not to kill but for the challenge."

"What are you talking about?" Jeff asked.

"You ever hear of Leopold and Loeb?" This time Will spoke more emphatically.

Both Karl and Jeff shook their heads. "Who were they?" Karl asked.

"Two guys who thought they were smart enough to commit the perfect murder. Back in the 1920s. But they got caught in twenty-four hours."

The other two men froze into silence.

"We're smarter," said Will presently. "Think of all the planning we'd have to do, a lot more than hunting deer or elk. And even without the murder it would be a helluva challenging game."

Silence, except for the fire, reigned for a while. Then Jeff said, "You *are* talking about a game, not a real murder, right?"

Will waved the hand holding his cigar. "The game would be the planning and stalking. Just like when we hunt deer. The kill hardly matters at that point. We only follow through because we want the meat and the rack. You can't hang a man's head on the wall."

That elicited a laugh from Karl. "True that." Even Jeff smiled after a moment.

"The most challenging game of all," Will continued. "How do we do it without leaving any evidence? How do we creep up on our prey?"

Karl snorted. "Men aren't as smart as deer, Will."

"But they're almost never alone."

After a bit, Jeff said, "Sorta like playing D&D when we were younger?"

"Like that," Will agreed. "Plotting and planning and stalking. That's all."

Presently all the men were sitting easily in their chairs and began to toss ideas around. If nothing else, it was an entertaining way to spend an icy evening.

Chapter One

Blaire Afton slept with the window cracked because she liked the cool night breeze, and the sounds of animals in the woods. As park ranger for the state of Wyoming, she supervised a forested area with a dozen scattered campgrounds and quite a few hiking trails, most all the camps and trails farther up the mountain.

Her cabin was also the main office, the entry point to the park, and her bedroom was upstairs in a loft. The breeze, chilly as it got at night, even in July, kept her from feeling closed in. The fresh air seemed to make her sleep deeper and more relaxed, as well.

It also seemed to keep away the nightmares that still occasionally plagued her. Ten months in Afghanistan had left their mark.

But tonight she was edgy as all get-out, and sleep stubbornly evaded her. Maybe just as well, she thought irritably. Nights when she felt like this often produced bad dreams, which in turn elicited worse memories.

Sitting up at last, she flipped on the fluorescent lantern beside her bed and dressed in her park ranger's uniform and laced up her boots. If sleep caught up with her finally, she could crash on the sofa downstairs. Right now, however, early coffee was sounding delicious.

There was absolutely no way she could make her boots silent on the open wooden staircase, but it didn't matter. All her staff were home for the night and she could bother only herself. Right now, bothering herself seemed like a fairly good idea.

The electric lines reached the cabin, having been run up the side of this mountain by the state, along with a phone landline that extended out to all the campgrounds in case of emergencies. Neither was perfectly reliable, but when they worked, they were a boon. Especially the electricity. Phone calls about vacant campsites didn't light up her life, nor did some of the stupid ones she received. Want a weather report? Then turn on the weather.

"Ha," she said aloud. The good news was that she had electric power this night. She walked over to her precious espresso machine and turned it on. A few shots over ice with milk and artificial sweetener...oh, yeah.

And since she was wide awake and had the

power, maybe she should check her computer and see if she had internet, as well. Monthly reports were due soon, and if she had to be awake, she might as well deal with them. Reports weren't her favorite part of this job, and sometimes she wondered if some of them had been created by a higher-up who just wanted to be important.

When her coffee was ready and filling her insulated mug, she decided to step outside and enjoy some of the night's unique quiet. It wasn't silent, but it was so different from the busier daylight hours. Tilting her head back, she could see stars overhead, bright and distant this nearly moonless night. The silvery glow was just enough to see by, but not enough to wash out the stars.

Sipping her coffee, she allowed herself to enjoy being out in the dark without fear. It might come back at any moment, but as Afghanistan faded further into her past, it happened much less often. She was grateful for the incremental improvement.

Grateful, too, that the head forester at the national forest abutting her state land was also a veteran, someone she could talk to. Gus Maddox guarded a longer past in combat than she did, and there was still a lot he wouldn't, or couldn't, talk about. But he'd been in special operations, and much of what they did remained secret for years.

In her case, her service had been more ordinary. Guarding supply convoys sounded tame until you learned they were a desirable target. She and her team had more than once found themselves in intense firefights, or the object of roadside bombs.

She shook herself, refusing to let memory intrude on this night. It was lovely and deserved its due. An owl hooted from deep within the woods, a lonely yet beautiful sound. All kinds of small critters would be scurrying around, trying to evade notice by running from hiding place to hiding place while they searched for food. Nature had a balance and it wasn't always pretty, but unlike war it served a necessary purpose.

Dawn would be here soon, and she decided to wait in hope she might see a cloud of bats returning to their cave three miles north. They didn't often fly overhead here, but occasionally she enjoyed the treat.

Currently there was a great deal of worry among biologists about a fungus that was attacking the little brown bat. She hoped they managed to save the species.

A loud report unexpectedly shattered the night. The entire world seemed to freeze. Only the gentle sigh of the night breeze remained as wildlife paused in recognition of a threat.

Blaire froze, too. She knew the sound of a gunshot. She also knew that no one was supposed to be hunting during the night or during this season.

What the hell? She couldn't even tell exactly where it came from. The sound had echoed off the rocks and slopes of the mountain. As quiet as the night was, it might have come from miles away.

Fifteen minutes later, the phone in her cabin started to ring.

Her heart sank.

TEN MILES SOUTH in his cabin in the national forest, August Maddox, Gus to everyone, was also enduring a restless night. Darkness had two sides to it, one favorable and one threatening, depending. In spec ops, he'd favored it when he was on a stealthy mission and didn't want to be detected. At other times, when he and his men were the prey, he hated it. The protection it sometimes afforded his troops could transform into deadliness in an instant.

As a result, he endured an ongoing battle with night. Time was improving it, but on nights like this when sleep eluded him, he sometimes forced himself to step outside, allowing the inkiness to swallow him, standing fast against urges to take cover. He hated this in himself, felt it as an ugly, inexcusable weakness, but hating it didn't make it go away.

The fingernail moon provided a little light,

and he used it to go around the side of the building to visit the three horses in the corral there. His own gelding, Scrappy, immediately stirred from whatever sleep he'd been enjoying and came to the rail to accept a few pats and nuzzle Gus in return.

Sometimes Gus thought the horse was the only living being who understood him. *Probably because Scrappy couldn't talk*, he often added in attempted lightness.

But Scrappy did talk in his own way. He could communicate quite a bit with a toss of his head or a flick of his tail, not to mention the pawing of his feet. Tonight the horse seemed peaceful, though, and leaned into his hand as if trying to share the comfort.

He should have brought a carrot, Gus thought. Stroking the horse's neck, he asked, "Who gave you that silly name, Scrappy?"

Of course the horse couldn't answer, and Gus had never met anyone who could. The name had come attached to the animal, and no one had ever changed it. Which was okay, because Gus kind of liked it. Unusual. He was quite sure the word hadn't been attached to another horse anywhere. It also made him wonder about the horse's coltish days five or six years ago.

Scrappy was a gorgeous, large pinto whose lines suggested Arabian somewhere in the past. He was surefooted in these mountains, though, which was far more important than speed. And he was evidently an animal who attached himself firmly, because Gus had found that when Scrappy was out of the corral, he'd follow Gus around more like a puppy than anything.

Right then, though, as Scrappy nudged his arm repeatedly, he realized the horse wanted to take a walk. It was dark, but not too dark, and there was a good trail leading north toward the state park lands.

And Blaire Afton.

Gus half smiled at himself as he ran his fingers through Scrappy's mane. Blaire. She'd assumed her ranger position over there about two years ago, and they'd become friends. Well, as much as two wary vets could. Coffee, conversation, even some good laughs. Occasional confidences about so-called reentry problems. After two years, Scrappy probably knew the path by heart.

But it was odd for the horse to want to walk in the middle of the night. Horses *did* sleep. But maybe Gus's restlessness had reached him and made him restless, as well. Or maybe he sensed something in the night. Prickles of apprehension, never far away in the dark, ran up Gus's spine.

"Okay, a short ride," he told Scrappy. "Just enough to work out a kink or two."

An internal kink. Or a thousand. Gus had given up wondering just how many kinks he'd brought home with him after nearly twenty years in the Army, most of it in covert missions. The grenade that had messed him up with shrapnel hadn't left as many scars as memory. Or so he thought.

He was tempted to ride bareback, given that he didn't intend to go far, but he knew better. As steady as Scrappy was, if he startled or stumbled Gus could wind up on the ground. Better to have the security of a saddle than risk an injury.

Entering the corral, he saw happiness in Scrappy's sudden prance. The other two horses roused enough to glance over, then went back to snoozing. They never let the night rambles disturb them. The other two horses apparently considered them to be a matter between Scrappy and Gus.

Shortly he led the freshly saddled Scrappy out of the corral. Not that he needed leading. He followed him over to the door of his cabin where a whiteboard for messages was tacked and he scrawled that he'd gone for a ride on the Forked Rivers Trail. A safety precaution in case he wasn't back by the time his staff started wandering in from their various posts. Hard-and-fast rule: never go into the forest without letting the rangers know where you were headed and when you expected to return. It applied to him as well as their guests.

Then he swung up into the saddle, listening to

Scrappy's happy nicker, enjoying his brief sideways prance of pleasure. And just like the song, the horse knew the way.

Funny thing to drift through his mind at that moment. A memory from childhood that seemed so far away now he wasn't sure it had really happened. Sitting in the car with his parents on the way to Grandmother's house. Seriously. Two kids in the back seat singing "Over the River" until his mother begged for mercy. His folks were gone now, taken by the flu of all things, and his sister who had followed him into the Army had been brought home in a box from Iraq.

Given his feelings about the darkness, it struck him as weird that the song and the attendant memories had popped up. But he ought to know by now how oddly the brain could work.

Scrappy's hooves were nearly silent on the pine needles that coated the trail. The duff under the trees was deep in these parts, and he'd suggested to HQ that they might need to clean up some of it. Fire hazard, and it hadn't rained in a while, although they were due for some soon to judge by the forecast. Good. They needed it.

The slow ride through the night woods was nearly magical. The creak of leather and the jingle of the rings on the bridle were quiet, but part of the feeling of the night. When he'd been in Germany he'd learned the story of the Christmas tree. The idea had begun with early and long winter nights, as travelers between villages had needed illumination to see their way. At some point people had started putting candles on tree branches.

Damn, he'd moved from Thanksgiving to Christmas in a matter of minutes and it was July. What the hell was going on inside his mind?

He shook his head a bit, then noticed that Scrappy was starting to get edgy himself. He was tossing his head an awful lot. What had he sensed on the night breeze? Some odor that bothered him. That could be almost anything out of the ordinary.

But the horse's reaction put him on high alert, too. Something was wrong with the woods tonight. Scrappy felt it and he wasn't one to question an animal's instincts and senses.

Worry began to niggle at him. They were getting ever closer to Blaire Afton's cabin. Could she be sick or in trouble?

Maybe it was an annoying guy thing, but he often didn't like the idea that she was alone there at night. In the national forest there were people around whom he could radio if he needed to, who'd be there soon if he wanted them. Blaire had no such thing going for her. Her employees were all on daylight hours, gone in the evening, not returning until morning. Budget, he supposed. Money was tight for damn near everything now.

Blaire would probably laugh in his face if she ever guessed he sometimes worried about her being alone out here. She had some of the best training in the world. If asked he'd say that he felt sorry for anyone who tangled with her.

But she was still alone there in that cabin, and worse, she was alone with her nightmares. Like him. He knew all about that.

Scrappy tossed his head more emphatically and Gus loosened the reins. "Okay, man, do your thing."

Scrappy needed no other encouragement. His pace quickened dramatically.

Well, maybe Blaire would be restless tonight, too, and they could share morning coffee and conversation. It was gradually becoming his favorite way to start a day.

Then he heard the unmistakable sound of a gunshot, ringing through the forest. At a distance, but he still shouldn't be hearing it. Not at this time of year. Not in the dark.

"Scrappy, let's go." He touched the horse lightly with his heels, not wanting him to break into a gallop that could bring him to harm, but just to hurry a bit.

Scrappy needed no further urging.

"WE THINK SOMEONE'S been shot."

The words that had come across the telephone

seemed to shriek in Blaire's ears as she hurried to grab a light jacket and her pistol belt as well as a shotgun out of the locked cabinet. On the way out the door she grabbed the first-aid kit. The sheriff would be sending a car or two, but she had the edge in time and distance. She would definitely arrive first.

The call had come from the most remote campground, and she'd be able to get only partway there in the truck. The last mile or so would have to be covered on the all-terrain side-by-side lashed to the bed of the truck.

If someone was injured, why had it had to happen at the most out-of-the-way campground? A campground limited to people who seriously wanted to rough it, who didn't mind carrying in supplies and tents. After the road ended up there, at the place she'd leave her truck, no vehicles of any kind were allowed. She was the only one permitted to head in there on any motorized vehicle. She had one equipped for emergency transport.

She was just loading the last items into her vehicle when Gus appeared, astride Scrappy, a welcome sight.

"I heard the shot. What happened?"

"Up at the Twin Rocks Campground. I just got a call. They think someone's been shot."

"Think?"

"That's the word. You want to follow me on horseback, or ride with me?" It never once entered her head that he wouldn't want to come along to help.

IT NEVER ENTERED his head, either. "I'm not armed," he warned her as he slipped off the saddle.

"We can share."

He loosely draped Scrappy's reins around the porch railing in front of the cabin, knowing they wouldn't hold him. He didn't want them to. It was a signal to Scrappy to hang around, not remain frozen in place. A few seconds later, he climbed into the pickup with Blaire and they started up the less-than-ideal road. He was glad his teeth weren't loose because Blaire wasted no time avoiding the ruts.

He spoke, raising his voice a bit to be heard over the roaring engine. "Have you thought yet about what you're doing for Christmas and Thanksgiving?"

She didn't answer for a moment as she shifted into a lower gear for the steepening road. "It's July. What brought that on?"

"Danged if I know," he admitted. "I was riding Scrappy in your direction because I'm restless tonight and it all started with a line from 'Over the River' popping into my head. Then as I was coming down the path I remembered how in the

Middle Ages people put candles on tree branches on long winter nights so the pathways would be lit for travelers. Which led to..."

"Christmas," she said. "Got it. Still weird."

He laughed. "That's what I thought, too. My head apparently plays by its own rules."

It was her turn to laugh, a short mirthless sound. "No kidding. I don't have to tell you about mine."

No, she didn't, and he was damned sorry that she carried those burdens, too. "So, holidays," he repeated. No point in thinking about what lay ahead of them. If someone had been shot, they both knew it wasn't going to be pretty. And both of them had seen it before.

"I'll probably stay right here," she answered. "I love it when the forest is buried in snow, and someone has to be around if the snowshoe hikers and the cross-country skiers get into trouble."

"Always," he agreed. "And doesn't someone always get into trouble?"

"From what I understand, it hasn't failed yet."

He drummed his fingers on his thigh, then asked, "You called the sheriff?"

"Yeah, but discharge of a weapon is in my bailiwick. They have a couple of cars heading this way. If I find out someone *has* been shot, I'll warn them. Otherwise I'll tell them to stand down."

Made sense. This wasn't a war zone after all.

Most likely someone had brought a gun along for protection and had fired it into the night for no good reason. Scared? A big shadow hovering in the trees?

And in the dead of night, wakened from a sound sleep by a gunshot, a camper could be forgiven for calling to say that someone *had* been shot even without seeing it. The more isolated a person felt, the more he or she was apt to expect the worst. Those guys up there at Twin Rocks were about as isolated as anyone could get without hiking off alone.

He hoped that was all it was. An accident that had been misinterpreted. His stomach, though, gave one huge twist, preparing him for the worst.

"You hanging around for the holidays?" she asked. Her voice bobbled as the road became rougher.

"Last year my assistant did," he reminded her. "This year it's me. What did you do last year?"

"Went to visit my mother in the nursing home. I told you she has Alzheimer's."

"Yeah. That's sad."

"Pointless to visit. She doesn't even recognize my voice on the phone anymore. Regardless, I don't think she feels lonely."

"Why's that?"

"She spends a lot of time talking to friends and relatives who died back when. Her own little party."

"I hope it comforts her."

"Me, too." Swinging a hard left, she turned onto a narrower leg of road that led directly to a dirt and gravel parking lot of sorts. It was where the campers left their vehicles before hiking in.

"You ever been to this campground?" she asked as she set the brake and switched off the ignition.

"Not on purpose," he admitted. "I may have. Scrappy and I sometimes wander a bit when we're out for a day-off ride."

"Everything has to be lugged in," she replied, as if that would explain all he needed to know.

It actually did. *Rustic* was the popular word for it. "They have a phone, though?"

"Yeah, a direct line to me. The state splurged. I would guess lawyers had something to do with that."

He gave a short laugh. "Wouldn't surprise me."

Even though Blaire was clearly experienced at getting the side-by-side off the back of her truck, he helped. It was heavy, it needed to roll down a ramp, and it might decide to just keep going.

Once it was safely parked, he helped reload the ramp and close the tailgate. Then there was loading the first-aid supplies and guns. She knew where everything went, so he took directions.

With a pause as he saw the roll of crime scene tape and box of latex gloves. And shoe covers. God. A couple of flashlights that would turn night into day. He hoped they didn't need any of it. Not any of it.

At least the state hadn't stinted on the side-by-side. It had a roof for rainy weather, and a roll bar he could easily grab for stability. There were four-point harnesses as well, no guarantee against every danger but far better than being flung from the vehicle.

These side-by-side UTVs weren't as stable as three-wheelers, either. It might be necessary for her job, but if he were out for joyriding, he'd vastly prefer a standard ATV.

She drove but tempered urgency with decent caution. The headlights were good enough, but this classified more as a migratory path than a road. Even knowing a ranger might have to get out here in an emergency, no one had wanted to make this campground easily accessible by vehicle. There were lots of places like that in his part of the forest. Places where he needed to drag teams on foot when someone got injured.

Soon, however, he saw the occasional glint of light through the trees. A lot of very-awake campers, he imagined. Frightened by the gunshot. He hoped they weren't frightened by more.

The forest thinned out almost abruptly as they reached the campground. He could make out scattered tents, well separated in the trees. Impossible in the dark to tell how many there might be.

But a group of people, all of whom looked as if they'd dragged on jeans, shirts and boots in a hurry, huddled together, a couple of the women hugging themselves.

Blaire brought the ATV to a halt, parked it and jumped off. He followed more slowly, not wanting to reduce her authority in any way. She was the boss here. He was just a visitor. And he wasn't so stupid that he hadn't noticed how people tended to turn to the man who was present first.

He waited by the vehicle as Blaire covered the twenty or so feet to the huddle. Soon excited voices reached him, all of them talking at the same time about the single gunshot that had torn the silence of the night. From the gestures, he guessed they were pointing to where they thought the shot came from, and, of course, there were at least as many directions as people.

They'd been in tents, though, and that would muffle the sound. Plus there were enough rocks around her to cause confusing echoes.

But then one man silenced them all.

"Mark Jasper didn't come out of his tent. His kid was crying just a few minutes ago, but then he quieted."

He saw Blaire grow absolutely still. "His kid?"

"He brought his four-year-old with him. I guess the shot may have scared him. But... Why didn't Mark come out?"

Good question, thought Gus. Excellent question.

"Maybe he didn't want to take a chance and expose his boy. They might have gone back to sleep," said one of the women. Her voice trembled. She didn't believe that, Gus realized.

Blaire turned slowly toward the tent that the man had pointed out. She didn't want to look. He didn't, either. But as she took her first step toward the shelter, he stepped over and joined her. To hell with jurisdiction. His gorge was rising. A kid had been in that tent? No dad joining the others? By now this Jasper guy could have heard enough of the voices to know it was safe.

He glanced at Blaire and saw that her face had set into lines of stone. She knew, too. When they reached the door of the tent, she stopped and pointed. Leaning over, he saw it, too. The tent was unzipped by about six or seven inches.

"Gloves," he said immediately.

"Yes."

Protect the evidence. The opening might have been left by this Jasper guy, or it might have been created by someone else. Either way...

He brought her a pair of latex gloves, then snapped his own set on. Their eyes met, and hers reflected the trepidation he was feeling.

Then he heard a sound from behind him and swung around. The guy who had announced that Jasper hadn't come out had followed them. "Back up, sir." His tone was one of command, honed by years of military practice.

"Now," Blaire added, the same steely note in her voice. "You might be trampling evidence."

The guy's eyes widened and he started to back up.

Now Blaire turned her head. "Carefully," she said sharply. "Don't scuff. You might bury something."

The view of the guy raising his legs carefully with each step might have been amusing under other circumstances. There was no amusement now.

"Ready?" Blaire asked.

"Yup."

She leaned toward the tent and called, "Mr. Jasper? I'm the ranger. We're coming in. We need to check on you." No sound answered her.

"Like anyone can be ready for this," she muttered under her breath as she reached up for the zipper tab. The metal teeth seemed loud as the world held its breath.

When she had the zipper halfway down, she parted the canvas and shone her flashlight inside.

"Oh, my God," she breathed.

Chapter Two

Blaire had seen a lot of truly horrible things during her time in Afghanistan. There had even
been times when she'd been nearly frozen by
a desire not to do what she needed to do. She'd
survived, she'd acted and on a couple of occa-
sions, she'd even saved lives.

This was different. In the glare of the flashlight she saw a man in a sleeping bag, his head
near the front opening. Or rather what was left of
his head. Worse, she saw a small child clinging
desperately to the man's waist, eyes wide with
shock and terror. That kid couldn't possibly understand this horror but had still entered the icy
pit of not being able to move, of hanging on to
his daddy for comfort and finding no response.

She squeezed her eyes shut for just a moment,
then said quietly to Gus, "The father's been shot
in the head. Dead. The kid is clinging to him and
terrified out of his mind. I need the boy's name."

Gus slipped away, and soon she heard him murmuring to the gathered campers.

Not knowing if she would ever get the boy's name, she said quietly, "Wanna come outside? I'm sort of like police, you know. You probably saw me working when you were on your way up here."

No response.

Then Gus's voice in her ear. "Jimmy. He's Jimmy."

"Okay." She lowered the zipper more. When Gus squatted, she let him continue pulling it down so she didn't have to take eyes off the frightened and confused little boy. "Jimmy? Would you like to go home to Mommy? We can get Mommy to come for you."

His eyes flickered a bit. He'd heard her.

"My friend Gus here has a horse, too. You want to ride a horse? His name is Scrappy and he's neat. All different colors."

She had his attention now and stepped carefully through the flap, totally avoiding the father. She wondered how much evidence she was destroying but didn't much care. The priority was getting that child out of there.

The floor of the tent was small and not easy to cross. A small sleeping bag lay bunched up, a trap for the unwary foot. Toys were scattered about, too, plastic horses, some metal and plastic cars and a huge metal tractor. She bet Jimmy had had fun making roads in the pine needles and duff outside.

As soon as she got near, she squatted. His gaze was focusing on her more and more, coming out of the shock and into the moment. "I think we need to go find your mommy, don't you?"

"Daddy?"

"We'll take care of Daddy for you, okay? Mommy is going to need you, Jimmy. She probably misses you so bad right now. Let's go and I'll put you on my ATV. You like ATVs?"

"Zoom." The smallest of smiles cracked his frozen face.

"Well, this is a big one, and it definitely zooms. It's also a little like riding a roller coaster. Come on, let's go check it out."

At last Jimmy uncoiled and stood. But there was no way Blaire was going to let him see any more of his father. She scooped him up in her arms and turned so that he'd have to look through her.

"Gus?"

"Yo."

"Could you hold the flap open, please?"

Who knew a skinny four-year-old could feel at once so heavy and light? The flashlight she carried wasn't helping, either. She wished she had a third arm.

"Are you cold, Jimmy?" she asked as she

moved toward the opening and bent a little to ease them through.

"A little bit," he admitted.

"Well, I've got a nice warm blanket on my ATV. You can curl up with it while I call your mommy, okay?" Lying. How was she going to call this kid's mother? Not immediately, for sure. She couldn't touch the corpse or look for ID until after the crime techs were done.

"Gus? The sheriff?"

"I radioed. There's a lot more than two cars on the way. Crime scene people, too."

"We've got to get this cordoned off."

"I'll ask Mr. Curious to help me. He'll love it. The kid?"

"Jimmy is going to get my favorite blanket and a place to curl up in the back of the ATV, right, Jimmy?"

Jimmy gave a small nod. His fingers dug into her, crumpling cloth and maybe even bruising a bit. She didn't care.

Walking carefully and slowly with the boy, almost unconsciously she began to hum a tune from her early childhood, "All Through the Night."

To her surprise, Jimmy knew the words and began to sing them with her. His voice was thin, frail from the shock, but he was clinging desperately to something familiar. After a moment, she began to sing softly with him. Before she reached the ATV, Jimmy's head was resting against her shoulder.

When the song ended, he said, "Mommy sings that." Then he started to sing it again.

And Blaire blinked hard, fighting back the first tears she'd felt in years.

GUS WATCHED BLAIRE carry the small child to the ATV. He'd already recovered the crime scene tape and there were plenty of trees to wind it around, but he hesitated for a moment, watching woman and child. He could imagine how hard this was for her, dealing with a freshly fatherless child. War did that too often. Now here, in a peaceful forest. Or one that should have been peaceful.

His radio crackled, and he answered it. "Maddox."

"We're about a mile out from the parking area," came the familiar voice of the sheriff, Gage Dalton. "Anything else we need to know?"

"I'm about to rope the scene right now. The vic has a small child. We're going to need some help with that and with finding a way to get in touch with family as soon as possible."

"We'll do what we can as fast as we can. The witnesses?"

"Some are trying to pack up. I'm going to stop that."

He was as good as his word, too. When he

clicked off the radio, he turned toward the people who had dispersed from the remaining knot and started to fold up tents.

"You all can stop right there. The sheriff will be here soon and you might be material witnesses. None of you can leave the scene until he tells you."

Some grumbles answered him, but poles and other items clattered to the ground. One woman, with her arms wrapped around herself, said, "I feel like a sitting duck."

"If you were," Gus said, "you'd already know it." That at least took some of the tension out of the small crowd. Then he signaled to the guy who'd tried to follow them to the tent and said, "You get to help me rope off the area."

The guy nodded. "I can do that. Sorry I got too close. Instinct."

"Instinct?"

"Yeah. Iraq. Know all the parameters of the situation."

Gus was familiar with that. He decided the guy wasn't a ghoul after all. He also proved to be very useful. In less than ten minutes, they had a large area around the victim's tent cordoned off. Part of him was disturbed that a gunshot had been heard but no one had approached the tent of the one person who hadn't joined them, not even the veteran. The tent in which a child had apparently been crying.

But it was the middle of the night, people had probably been wakened from a sound sleep and were experiencing some difficulty in putting the pieces together in any useful way. Camping was supposed to be a peaceful experience unless you ran into a bear. And, of course, the sound of the child crying might have persuaded them everything was okay in that tent. After all, it looked untouched from the outside.

Scared as some of these people were that there might be additional gunfire, they all might reasonably have assumed that Jasper and his son were staying cautiously out of sight.

Once he and Wes, the veteran, had roped off the area, there wasn't another thing they could do before the cops arrived. Preserve the scene, then stand back. And keep witnesses from leaving before they were dismissed by proper authority. He could understand, though, why some of them just wanted to get the hell out of here.

The fact remained, any one of that group of twelve to fourteen people could be the shooter. He wondered if any one of them had even considered that possibility.

Blaire settled Jimmy in the back of the ATV after moving a few items to the side. She had a thick wool blanket she carried in case she got stranded outside overnight without warning, and she did her best to turn it into a nest.

Then she pulled out a shiny survival blanket

and Jimmy's world seemed to settle once again. "Space blanket!" The excitement was clear in his voice.

"You bet," she said, summoning a smile. "Now just stay here while we try to get your mommy. If you do that for me, you can keep the space blanket."

That seemed to make him utterly happy. He snuggled into the gray wool blanket and hugged the silvery Mylar to his chin. "I'll sleep," he announced.

"Great idea," she said. She couldn't resist brushing his hair gently back from his forehead. "Pleasant dreams, Jimmy."

He was already falling asleep, though. Exhausted from his fear and his crying, the tyke was nodding off. "Mommy says that, too," he murmured. And then his thumb found its way into his mouth and his eyes stayed closed.

Blaire waited for a minute, hoping the child could sleep for a while but imagining the sheriff's arrival with all the people and the work they needed to do would probably wake him. She could hope not.

HE HADN'T KNOWN the kid was there. God in heaven, he hadn't known. Jeff scrambled as quietly as he could over rough ground, putting as much distance between him and the vic as he could.

He'd been shocked by the sight of the kid.
He almost couldn't bring himself to do it. If he
hadn't, though, he'd be the next one The Hunt
Club would take out. They'd warned him.

His damn fault for getting too curious. Now
he was on the hook with them for a murder he
didn't want to commit, and he was never going
to forget that little boy. Those eyes, those cries,
would haunt him forever.

Cussing viciously under his breath, he grabbed
rocks and slipped on scree. He couldn't even turn
on his flashlight yet, he was still too close. But
the moon had nose-dived behind the mountain
and he didn't even have its thin, watery light to
help him in his escape.

His heart was hammering and not just because
of his efforts at climbing. He'd just killed a man
and probably traumatized a kid for life. That kid
wasn't supposed to be there. He'd been watching the guy for the last two weeks and he'd been
camping solo. What had he done? Brought his
son up for the weekend? Must have.

Giving Jeff the shock of his life. He should
have backed off, should have told the others he
couldn't do it because the target wasn't alone.
Off-season. No tag. Whatever. Surely he could
have come up with an excuse so they'd have
given him another chance.

Maybe. Now that he knew what the others had
been up to, he couldn't even rely on their friend-

ship anymore. Look what they'd put him up to, even when he'd sworn he'd never rat them out.

And he wouldn't have. Man alive, he was in it up to his neck even if he hadn't known they were acting out some of the plans they'd made. An accomplice. He'd aided them. The noose would have tightened around his throat, too.

God, why hadn't he been able to make them see that? He wasn't an innocent who could just walk into a police station and say, "You know what my friends have been doing the last few years?"

Yeah. Right.

He swore again as a sharp rock bit right through his jeans and made him want to cry out from the unexpected pain. He shouldn't be struggling up the side of a mountain in the dark. He shouldn't be doing this at all.

He had believed it was all a game. A fun thing to talk about when they gathered at the lodge in the fall for their usual hunting trip. Planning early summer get-togethers to eyeball various campgrounds, looking for the places a shooter could escape without being seen.

The victim didn't much matter. Whoever was convenient and easy. The important thing was not to leave anything behind. To know the habits of the prey the same way they would know the habits of a deer.

Did the vic go hiking? If so, along what trails

and how often and for how long? Was he or she alone very often or at all? Then Will had gotten the idea that they should get them in their tents. When there were other people in the campground, making it so much more challenging. Yeah.

He had believed it was just talk. He'd accompanied the others on the scouting expeditions, enjoying being in the woods while there were still patches of snow under the trees. He liked scoping out the campgrounds as the first hardy outdoorsy types began to arrive. And that, he had believed, was where it ended.

Planning. Scouting. A game.

But he'd been so wrong he could hardly believe his own delusion. He'd known these guys all his life. How was it possible he'd never noticed the psychopathy in either of them? Because that's what he now believed it was. They didn't give a damn about anyone or anything except their own pleasure.

He paused to catch his breath and looked back over his shoulder. Far away, glimpsed through the thick forest, he caught sight of flashing red, blue and white lights. The police were there.

He'd known it wouldn't be long. That was part of the plan. Once he fired his gun, he had to clear out before the other campers emerged, and not long after them the cops.

Well, he'd accomplished that part of his task.

He was well away by the time the campers dared to start coming out. But the little kid's wails had followed him into the night.

Damn it!

So he'd managed to back out of the place without scuffing up the ground in a way that would mark his trail. No one would be able to follow him. But now he was mostly on rocky terrain and that gave him added invisibility.

The damn duff down there had been hard to clear without leaving a visible trail. It had helped that so many campers had been messing it around this summer, but still, if he'd dragged his foot or… Well, it didn't matter. He hadn't.

But then there had been the farther distances. Like where he had kept watch. His movements. Too far out for anyone to notice, of course. He'd made sure of that.

So he'd done everything right. They'd never catch him and the guys would leave him alone. That's all he wanted.

But he hated himself, too, and wished he'd been made of sterner stuff, the kind that would have gone to the cops rather than knuckle under to threats and the fear that he would be counted an accomplice to acts he hadn't committed.

Now there was no hope of escape for him or his soul. He'd done it. He'd killed a man. He was one of them, owned by them completely. Sold to the devil because of a threat to his life.

He feared, too, that if they were identified they would succeed in convincing the police that he was the killer in the other cases, that they were just his friends and he was pointing the finger at them to save his own hide.

Yeah, he had no trouble imagining them doing that, and doing it successfully. They'd plotted and planned so well that there was nothing to link *them* to the murders except him.

At last he made it over the ridge that would hide him from anyone below, not that the campground wasn't now concealed from view by thick woods.

But even if they decided to look around, they'd never find him now. All he had to do was crawl into the small cave below and await daylight. Then he would have a clear run to his car to get out of the forest.

All carefully planned. He'd be gone before any searcher could get up here.

Damn, he wanted a cigarette. But that had been part of their planning, too. No smoking. The tobacco smell would be distinctive, so they avoided it unless campfires were burning.

Who had come up with that idea?

He couldn't remember. He was past caring. He slid into the dark embrace of the cave at last, with only a short time before dawn.

Past caring. That was a good place to be. He

envied the others. Instead he kept company with the remembered cries of a young boy.

BLAIRE WISHED SHE could do more. She was the kind of person who always wanted to take action, to be useful, but right now the police were in charge, using skills she didn't have to look for evidence, so she kept an eye on the little boy in the bed of her ATV and on the scene where some officers were busy questioning other campers and the rest were busy photographing the scene and hunting for evidence. Pacing back and forth between the two locations, she imagined she was creating a rut.

At least Jimmy slept. She hoped he slept right through when they removed his father in a body bag. She hated the thought that such a scene might be stamped in his mind forever.

She knew all about indelible images. She wished sometimes for a version of brain bleach. Just rinse your head in it and the dark, ugly stuff would be washed away.

Nice wish. She was old enough, however, to realize how unrealistic such a wish was. Life was the accumulation of experiences, and you could only hope that you'd learn from all of them, good or bad.

Gus stayed close to the line, attentive as the officers questioned the witnesses. Dropping by from time to time, she heard the same story repeated by everyone. They'd been asleep. Awakened suddenly by the loud, sharp clap. At first they hadn't even been sure they'd heard it.

Some had sat up, waiting to see if it came again. Others considered rolling over and going back to sleep.

Then came the sound of Jimmy's crying. Yes, he sounded scared but that might be a reaction to the sudden, loud noise. He was with his father, so he'd be okay.

Only slowly had some come to the realization that perhaps they'd better look outside to see what had happened. By then there was nothing to see, and the night had been silent except for the little boy's sobbing.

Which again they ignored because he was with his father. Except for Wes.

"I was in Iraq. I'll never mistake a gunshot for anything else. When the boy kept crying, I knew. I just knew someone had been shot. Maybe suicide, I thought. I was the first one out of my tent. The others took another couple of minutes. Regardless, I'm the one who ran to the emergency phone and called the ranger. No, I didn't touch a thing."

Wes paused, looking down, saying quietly, "It was hell listening to that kid and not acting. But his dad might have been okay. My appearance might have just scared the boy more." His mouth twisted. "They don't make rules of engagement for this."

"I hear you," Gus said. Several deputies who were also vets murmured agreement.

The sheriff spoke. "You did the best thing."

Except, thought Blaire, she'd moved in, opened the tent, stepped inside and took the boy out. She'd interfered with the scene. Next would be her turn to be grilled.

By the time they came to her, however, they were allowing the others to pack up as long as they were willing to leave contact information with the deputies. The early morning sun cast enough light on the world that details had emerged from the night, giving everything more depth. Making the trees look aged and old and maybe even weary. But that might be her own state of mind. Usually the forest gave her a sense of peace, and the trees offered her a stately temple.

The sheriff, Gage Dalton, and one of his deputies, Cadell Marcus, she thought, joined her just outside the roped area.

"Yes," she said before they even asked, "I touched the front of the tent. I was wearing gloves. I pulled the zipper down partway, poked my flashlight in and saw the scene. I had to get the little boy out of there."

Dalton nodded. "Of course you did. So what did you first see as you approached?"

"The zipper was pulled down from the top. I don't know how familiar you are with camping gear, but these days you can get tents with zippers that open both ways. A top opening allows in air while keeping protection down low from small critters. Anyway, it was open six or seven inches. Then I opened it more."

She paused, closing her eyes, remembering. "I didn't think about it at the time, but the inner screen wasn't closed. Doesn't necessarily mean anything because we don't have much of a flying insect problem up here."

Gage nodded. "Okay."

Cadell was making notes.

"Anyway, almost as soon as I poked the flashlight in, I saw the victim and I saw his son clinging to him. My only thought at that point was to get the child out of there as fast as I could. I asked Gus to pull the zipper down the rest of the way. I entered, trying not to disturb anything, and picked the boy up. I carried him to my ATV, where he's sleeping now."

"Did you notice anything else?"

She shook her head and opened her eyes. "Frankly, once I saw that man's head, I was aware of nothing else but the little boy. I seem to recall some toys being scattered around, the boy was out of his sleeping bag which, if I remember correctly, was pretty balled up, and that's it. I was completely focused on removing the child while trying not to step on anything." She paused. "Oh. I turned so Jimmy wouldn't be able to see his father."

Gage surprised her by reaching out to pat her upper arm. "You did the right things. We just needed to know where any contamination might have come from."

"What about Jimmy?" she asked. Concern for the child, kept on simmer for the last couple of hours, now bubbled up like a pot boiling over.

"Sarah Ironheart has called child services. They're contacting the mother." He paused. "Do you think Jimmy trusts you?"

"Insofar as he can. He let me put him in my ATV to sleep." She smiled without humor. "I think the space blanket did it."

"Probably. I'm wondering, if I put you and him in the back of my car, we can take him to town to the social worker. His mom should be on the way."

She hesitated, hating to walk away from what was clearly her job. This campground was her responsibility, and once the cops left...

"Go ahead," said Gus. "I'll meet your staff when they arrive in the next hour and explain. I'm sure they can fill in for you."

The sheriff spoke. "And after the techs are done I'm leaving a couple of deputies up here so the scene won't be disturbed. You're covered."

He gave her a half smile as he said it.

"Yeah, CYA," she responded. "Okay." She couldn't bear the thought of waking Jimmy only to turn him over to a stranger without explanation. The car ride to town would give her plenty of opportunity to reassure him, and maybe by the time they reached Conard City his mom will have arrived.

She looked at Gus. "I promised him a horse ride."

"We might be able to work in a couple of minutes when we get to your HQ. If that's okay with Gage."

"Fine by me. That little boy needs everything good he can get right now."

Chapter Three

Jimmy woke quickly. At first he looked frightened but he recognized Blaire and when she told him they were going to take a ride in a police car, he seemed delighted. Not once, not yet, did he ask the dreaded question, "Where's my daddy?"

They sat in the back of Gage's official SUV and Gage obliged him by turning on the rack of lights but explained people in the woods were still sleeping so he couldn't turn on the siren.

Jimmy appeared satisfied with that. Then Blaire began the onerous task of explaining to him that they were taking him to his mom and finally he asked, "Where's my daddy?"

Her heart sank like a stone. How the hell did you explain this to a four-year-old? It wasn't her place. He'd need his mom and a social worker for this.

She cleared her throat. "He can't come with us right now."

After a moment, Jimmy nodded. "He's helping the police, right?"

She couldn't bring herself to answer and was grateful when he didn't press the issue, apparently satisfied with his own answer.

Which gave her plenty of time to contemplate the kind of monster who would shoot a man while his young son was nearby. Only in battle when her comrades were in danger had she ever felt a need to kill, but she felt it right then and memories surged in her, the past burst into the present and she wanted to vomit.

But Jimmy fell asleep and they sailed right past her headquarters building without offering him the promised horse ride. Gus, who had been following them down, pulled over and gave a hands-up signal as they drove past. Letting her know he'd figured it out.

It was good of him to offer to stay and inform her staff what was going on. She could hardly stop to call and radio, and she couldn't wait for them herself, not with this trusting, precious little boy cuddled up against her.

Just as well. She wasn't sure what world she was inhabiting. Afghanistan? Conard County? The state park? Images, like mixed-up slides, kept flashing in her mind and she had to make a huge effort to focus on the back of Gage's head, on the fact she was in his vehicle. On the boy curled against her so trustingly.

That trust was killing her. Nobody should trust her like that. Not him most especially. He was just a kid and when he found out and finally understood what had happened, he might never trust another soul in his life.

Almost without realizing it, as the town grew closer and the day grew brighter, she was making a silent promise to herself. Somehow she was going to find the SOB who'd done this. If the cops didn't get him first, she wasn't going to give up the hunt.

Because someone deserved to pay for this. Someone deserved to die.

MILES AWAY, THE killer was hotfooting it down a mountainside to his vehicle. The cries of the child rang loud in his head and he thought bitterly that he should have just kidnapped the kid and carried him along.

He'd been angry at his friends. He'd been scared of them, maybe even terrified. But now he loathed them. He wished he could find a way to get even that wouldn't involve putting himself in prison for life.

Thoughts of revenge fueled him as he raced toward safety.

GUS HAD LOADED the ATV onto Blaire's truck and brought everything down to her HQ, where he waited patiently. As staff members reported for their day's work, he explained what had happened and told them to avoid the upper campground, so they wouldn't get in the way of the police.

While he was telling them, an ambulance brought the body down. Silence fell among the six men and women who were about to fan out to their various jobs. They stood, watching it pass, and for several long minutes, no one spoke.

Then Gus's radio crackled. It was one of his own staff.

"You coming back today, Gus, or you want me to stand in?"

"I'm not sure." He was thinking of Blaire. She might need more than a cup of coffee after this. "You take over, Josh. I'll let you know what's up."

"Terrible thing," Josh said. "You can bet we're going to be on high alert today."

"Good. We don't know which direction the perp took off when he left. Or whether he'll shoot again."

That made the local crew shift nervously and eye him. *Oh, hell,* he thought. He'd just messed up everything. What could he say? He couldn't very well send them out to patrol the other campgrounds. Not after this. They were seasonal workers, not trained for this kind of thing. And he was still more used to talking to other soldiers than civilians. He needed to guard his tongue.

"You got stuff you can do nearby?" he asked, scanning them.

One spoke. "Blaire's been talking about replacing the fire rings at the Cottonwood Campground."

"Nearby?"

"Yeah."

"Then do that."

"We'll need the truck to cart the concrete and the rings."

Gus nodded. "Okay. Good idea. Stick together. I'm almost positive the threat is gone, though."

"I'll feel better tomorrow," one said sarcastically.

He helped them unload the ATV, then fill the truck bed with bags of concrete and steel fire rings. Finally, he turned over the keys and watched them drive away. East. Away from the campground where the shooting had occurred. Not that he could blame them.

Then he went inside and made a fresh pot of coffee. He eyed the espresso machine because he loved Blaire's espresso, but he didn't know how to use it. Maybe he'd remedy that when she got back, ask for instructions.

While he waited for the coffee he went outside and whistled for Scrappy. Five minutes later, the gelding emerged from the woods to the north, looking quite perky. He must have picked up some sleep during all the uproar.

When the horse reached him, he patted his neck, then was astonished—he was always astonished when it happened—when Scrappy wrapped his neck around him, giving him a hug.

The horse was a mind reader? No, a mood reader. He patted and stroked Scrappy until the horse needed to move and pranced away.

"You getting hungry?"

Scrappy bobbed his head emphatically. If that horse could talk...

He had some feed in one of the saddlebags and put it on the edge of the porch, making sure Scrappy's reins wouldn't get in his way. Water. He needed water, too.

He went back inside and looked around until he found a big bucket in a supply closet. That would do.

A little while later, cup of coffee in his hand, he perched on the step of the small porch and shared breakfast with Scrappy. Maybe his best friend, he thought.

But his mind was wandering elsewhere, to Blaire, to the murder, to the little guy who'd lost his father.

It had been a while, thank God, since he'd felt murderous, but today was shaking him back into that old unwanted feeling.

A sleeping man. His child nearby. What kind of person would take that shot without a threat driving him? And how offensive could a sleeping man be? Kid aside, the killer had to be the worst kind of coward.

Afraid of where his thoughts might take him, because he'd spent a lot of time getting himself past the war, he forced himself to notice other things. The play of the light on the trees as the sun rose ever higher. The bird calls. Even more entertaining were the squirrels darting around, jumping from branch to branch and walking out on slender twigs, looking like high-wire daredevils. Even at times hanging upside down while they gnawed a branch. Weird, they usually did that only in the spring and fall.

BLAIRE RETURNED IN the late morning, looking absolutely wrung out. A police vehicle dropped her off, then turned around and headed back down the mountain. Gus rose as she approached, but she lowered herself to the porch step, eyeing Scrappy, who'd found a clump of grass to investigate.

"You must want to get back," she said.

"I most likely want to get you a cup of coffee. Regular because I don't know how your espresso machine works." He lowered himself beside her and asked, "Awful?"

"Awful," she agreed. "That poor little boy. At least his mother was already there when we arrived. But then he asked the question he didn't ask before."

"What's that?"

"Where's Daddy?"

"Oh. My. God." Gus didn't even want to imagine it, but his mind threw it up in full view, inescapable.

"Yeah." She sighed, leaned against the porch stanchion and closed her eyes.

"Your crew is out working on fire rings at Cottonwood. They didn't seem too eager to split up."

Her eyes opened to half-mast. "I don't imagine they would. I'm not too eager myself. God, what a monster, and it's too soon to hope he's made his way to the far ends of the Earth. He could be hanging around out there."

He couldn't deny it. "Look, we've both been up most of the night. If you want to sleep, I'll stand guard here until your people are done for the day. If not, let me get you some coffee."

"Coffee sounds good," she admitted. "I may be overtired, but I'm too wound up to sleep. What I really want is to wrap my hands around someone's throat. A specific someone."

He could identify with that. He'd just finished brewing a second pot of coffee so he was able to bring her a piping mug that smelled rich and fresh. He brought one for himself and sat beside her once again.

"I'm still trying to wrap my mind around the kind of person who would do something like that," she said. "It had to be in cold blood. Nothing had happened as far as anyone knows."

"His wife?"

"She's already been gently questioned. Nobody who'd want to kill him, nobody who'd had a fight with him recently, Gage told me."

"Well, great. The trail is awfully lean."

"If it's there at all." She sighed and sipped her coffee. "You must need to get back."

"My assistant is filling in. Unless you want to get rid of me, I'm here for now."

She turned her head, looking straight at him for the first time, and he noted how hollow her eyes looked. "Thanks. I'm not keen on being alone right now."

"Then there's no need." He paused. "We've shared a whole lot over cups of joe."

"That we have." She tilted her head back and drew several deep breaths as if drinking in the fresh woodland scents. "I'll share something with you right now. If the police don't have much success quickly, I'm going to start a search of my own. I know these woods like the back of my hand. He can't have come in and out without leaving some trace."

He turned his mug in his hands, thinking about it. "You're right. If it comes to that, I'll help you. But we can't wait too long. One rain and everything will be lost."

"Yeah." Again she raised her coffee to her lips,

and this time she nearly drained the mug. Rising, she put her foot on the step. "I need more caffeine. If you want, I'll make espresso."

"Only if I can watch and learn. Then you'll never get rid of me."

That at least drew a weak laugh from her. Once inside, he leaned against the narrow counter with his arms folded and watched her make the beverage. From time to time she told him things that wouldn't be immediately obvious, like turning the handled filter to one side to create the pressure.

"Espresso has to be brewed under pressure."

But her mind was obviously elsewhere, and to be frank, so was his.

"People get murdered," she remarked as she finished and handed him a tall cup holding three shots. "Doctor as you like. Ice in the freezer, thank God, milk in the fridge, sweetener in these little packets."

"Ice will water it down," he remarked.

"Yeah, but I like mine cold unless it's winter. Your choice."

He went for the ice, saying, "People get murdered... But what? You didn't finish that thought."

"No, I didn't." Her own cup in hand, she scooped ice into it and topped it with milk. "People get murdered, but not often by strangers while sleeping in a tent with their little son."

"Agreed."

"Outside?" she asked.

"I hate being stuck indoors." Another leftover from years in the military. He never felt all that safe when four walls held him and cut off his view.

They returned to the front steps. Scrappy looked almost as if he were sleeping standing up. Usually, he curled up on the ground, but not today. The tension the two of them were feeling must be reaching him, as well.

"I like your horse," she remarked. "Wish I could have one."

"Then get one."

"It's not in my nonexistent budget. And I don't get paid enough to afford one. Besides, I'm so shackled by things I need to do he might not get enough exercise."

"You're even more understaffed than I am."

"No kidding."

It was easier to talk about budgets and staffing than what had happened during the wee hours this morning. He sipped his espresso, loving the caffeine kick because he was tired, too, from lack of sleep, and waited. There'd be more. They were both vets. Memories had been stirred up, especially for her because she'd had to see it all.

Yeah, there'd be more. Because she'd had to help the kid.

But as noon began to approach, she said nothing more, and he had nothing to say. He was cramming the memories back into the dark pit where they belonged and he decided she must be doing the same.

Unfortunately, burying them wasn't a permanent solution. Like zombies, they kept rising anew and they were never welcome. And sometimes, like zombies, they'd devour you whole and all you could do was hang on. Or give in because there was no fighting it.

He glanced down into his cup and realized he'd finished his espresso. He'd have liked some more but decided not to ask.

At long last she turned to look at him, for the first time that day her blue eyes looking almost as brilliant as the sunny western sky. "That kid is going to have problems. He may not have seen the mess, he may not understand what happened, but he would remember that he left his dad behind in a tent on a mountainside. His mom will tell him about it later, but he's going to remember leaving his dad."

Gus nodded. "Yeah, he will." Of that he was certain. "The question will be whether he believes he abandoned his father."

She nodded and looked down at the mug she held. "More espresso?"

"I'd like that."

Those blue eyes lifted again. "You sure you don't have to get back?"

"Not today. I have a good staff. But even so, I'm in no rush to face the inevitable questions about what happened over here."

"Me neither." Her eyes shuttered briefly. "So my crew are out replacing fire rings?"

He'd told her that but under the circumstances didn't feel she'd slipped a memory cog. Overload. She must be experiencing it. "Yeah, it was the first thing they thought to do when I explained what had happened. Besides, I exceeded my authority."

Her head snapped around to look at him again. "Meaning?"

"I suggested today would be a good day to stick together."

After a few beats, she nodded. "You're right. I didn't even think of that. The creep could still be out there."

"I don't think there's any question that he's still out there. The only question is, did he leave the forest or is he hanging out somewhere?"

Her charming, crooked smile peeked out. "Correcting my precision now?"

He flashed a smile back at her. "You know why."

Of course she knew why. With a sigh, she rose. "Let's go make some more coffee. If I tried to sleep I wouldn't rest anyway, so I might as well be wired."

Inside the cabin was dim. Because of the

harsh, cold winters, the builders hadn't been generous with windows except at the very front where visitors would enter. Consequently, the rear room that housed the small kitchen and dining area was dim and needed the lights turned on. Blaire flipped the switch, then turned on the espresso maker.

"How many shots?" she asked Gus.

"It's funny, but I'm not used to thinking of coffee in terms of shots."

That drew a faint laugh from her. She picked up and wagged a double shot glass at him. "How many of these?"

He laughed outright. "Okay, two."

She nodded and turned back to the machine.

"You gonna be okay?" he asked as the pump began pushing water through the coffee grounds. Noisy thing.

"Sure," she said, leaning against the counter and watching the espresso pour into the double shot glass. "I'm always okay. It's not necessarily pleasant, but I'm okay."

Yeah, *okay* was a long way from being happy, content or otherwise good. He shook his head a little and pulled out one of the two chairs at the small table, sitting while he watched her. "This day is endless."

"What brought you this way this morning?"

"I was restless and couldn't sleep. Scrappy was

agitating for a ride so I decided to saddle up. I think he was feeling my mood."

"That wouldn't surprise me. Animals are very sensitive to energy, at least in my experience." She placed his mug in front of him again. "You know where the fixins are."

Making himself at home in her kitchen felt right. At least at the moment. He dressed up his espresso and waited for her to make her own. "Plans for today, since you can't sleep?"

"I'm probably going to run this morning like a broken record in my head." She finished pouring milk into her mug, added a few ice cubes, then turned. "Outside, if you don't mind. The walls are closing in."

He knew the feeling well. He held open the front door for her and resumed his perch on the step. She paced for a bit on the bare ground that probably served as a parking lot when people checked in and were directed to their campgrounds.

"I keep thinking," she said, "that the crime scene guys aren't going to find much that's useful. The ground was a mess, did you notice? People had obviously scuffed it up pretty good last night even if they didn't this morning."

"I saw," he said in agreement. "What are you thinking?"

"That this guy knew what he was doing. That

he didn't just walk into a random campsite and shoot someone through an opening in their tent."

He sat up a little straighter. He must have been more tired than he realized not to have thought of this himself. "You're saying stalking."

"I'm suggesting it, yes. No bumbling around in the dark as far as anyone knows. Certainly some of the people in the other tents must be light enough sleepers that they'd have heard activity."

"Maybe so." He was chewing the idea in his head.

"So, if he planned in advance he had to watch in advance. He'd have done that from a distance, right?"

He nodded. He'd done enough recon to know the drill. "Say he did."

"Then the cops might not find anything useful at the scene."

He nodded, sucking some air between his front teeth as his mouth tightened. "What are your plans for tomorrow? Got any time for reconnaissance?"

"I can make it."

"Can you ride?"

"Sure."

"So shall I borrow an extra mount or do you want to walk a perimeter first?"

She thought about it. "Walk," she decided. "We don't want to miss something."

"This assumes the cops don't find something today."

"Of course."

Their eyes met and the agreement was sealed. They'd do a little searching of their own.

That made him feel a bit better. He hoped it did for her, too.

THAT EVENING, JEFF pulled his car into the lodge's small parking area and went to face the music. He'd made a mistake and wished he could figure out a way of not telling Will and Karl. Desperately wished. Because things were going to get worse now.

But Jeff was acutely aware that he was a lousy liar. He could see them when they arrived tomorrow and pretend that everything had gone off without a hitch, but it wouldn't take them long to realize he was being untruthful.

The bane of his existence.

He let himself in and began to build a fire on the big stone hearth. That task was expected of the first to arrive, and given that the nights were chilly at this altitude, even in the summer when it had been known to snow occasionally, a small fire burning all the time was welcome.

The heavy log construction of the lodge acted

like an insulator, too. Once it had caught the chill, it hung on to it until it was driven out.

The others weren't expected until late tomorrow, though. Fine by him. There was plenty to eat and drink and maybe he could find a way to omit mentioning his oversight. His major oversight.

Besides, it might amount to nothing. One shell casing? How much could that tell anyone? That he'd used a hollow-point bullet in a .45? Lots of folks bought hollow points and even more owned .45s. Hollow points were less likely to pass through the target and cause collateral damage, while still inflicting far more damage on the target than a full metal jacket.

He couldn't have been sure what he'd be facing when he opened that tent a few inches, but he knew he wanted to kill his target without killing anything else.

They'd find the remains of the bullet at autopsy anyway. A popular brand that could be purchased in an awful lot of places. No, that wouldn't lead to him.

But the shell casing automatically ejected by his pistol? He should have scooped that up, but in his panic to get away, he'd clean forgotten it was lying on the ground. What if it had retained his fingerprints?

Not likely, he assured himself. The way he'd handled those bullets, any fingerprints should be just smears. The heat of the powder burning before it ejected the round from the shell should have wiped out any DNA evidence.

So yeah, he'd made a mistake. It wasn't a god-awful mistake, though. Hell, they couldn't necessarily even link it to the shooting, regardless of bullet fragments they might find at autopsy. No, because *anyone* could have been shooting out there at any time. That brass casing might be months old.

So no, it wasn't a catastrophe.

He spent a great deal of time that evening sipping beer and bucking himself up, dreading the moment tomorrow when his friends would come through the door.

Friends? He wasn't very sure of that any longer. Friends would have taken his word for it that he wouldn't squeal on them. Friends should have trusted him rather than threatening him.

Thinking about those threats put him in the blackest of moods. He wasn't a killer. He *wasn't*. He'd killed, though. In self-defense, he reminded himself. Because failing to take that guy out would have been signing his own death sentence. Yeah, self-defense, not murder.

That proved to be a small sop to his conscience, but he needed one. While the cries of the child had begun to fade to the background, the memory of them still made him supremely uncomfortable.

He'd caused that. Did self-defense justify that?

He hoped the kid was too young to understand what had happened.

Because he hated to think of the nightmares he'd caused if the kid wasn't.

Chapter Four

The morning was still dewy when Blaire awoke from troubled, uneasy dreams. At least she'd finally been able to crash after a day that had seemed like a nightmare that would never end, a day during which she'd become so exhausted she had often felt as if she were only slightly attached to her own body.

She'd had the feeling before, in combat and the aftermath, but not since then. Not until yesterday.

It hadn't just been lack of sleep that had gotten to her. Jimmy had gotten to her. He had caused her an emotional turmoil unlike any she had felt since one of her comrades had been hit in a firefight. Or blasted by a roadside bomb.

All she could remember was how he'd been crying and clinging to his dead father. Yeah, he'd perked up well enough after she'd carried him away, singing to him, and he loved the silvery blanket, but how much trauma had he endured?

How much had he understood and how much of that would stay with him forever?

She had no idea how good a four-year-old's long-term memory might be, but she suspected those memories were stronger if they carried a huge emotional impact. Heck, that was true for most people. Some events just got etched into your brain as if by acid.

Her staff showed up, trickling in around 8:00 a.m. The first thing they wanted to know was news about the shooting. She had none. Then they asked if they could keep working on the fire rings as they had yesterday.

Of course they could. It wasn't like the job hadn't been done, and from what she'd seen yesterday afternoon, she figured there was hardly a camper left in the park. When she climbed into her truck to check out all the sites, she found she was right: only one hardy camper remained, a guy who always spent nearly the entire summer here. He was friendly enough, but clearly didn't want to strike up any lengthy conversations. Most days he sat beside a small fire drinking coffee. Beans seemed to be his preferred meal. Sometimes he went fishing in the tumbling stream a couple of hundred yards behind his campsite, and she'd occasionally seen a couple of freshly cleaned fish on a frying pan over his small fire.

"Nothing better than fresh fish," she inevitably said.

"Nothing," he always agreed before they went their separate ways.

Finally, because she couldn't ignore it any longer, she drove up to the site of yesterday's horror. She left her truck in the small parking lot next to a sheriff's vehicle but eschewed her ATV. She needed the walk back to the site, needed to stretch her legs and try to clear the air. When she got there, she felt a whole lot better.

The deputies Gage had promised stood guard. Seeing them, she wished she'd thought to bring a thermos of soup or something with her. Their only seat was a fallen log outside the taped-off area, and neither of them looked as if they were having a good time.

"Boring duty, huh?" she asked as she approached. Her uniform identified her as theirs identified them. She couldn't remember having met either of them before. They looked almost brand spanking new. Together they formed a sea of khaki, hers interrupted with dark pants and a dark green quilted vest over her shirt. Both of the deputies looked as if they wished they'd brought a vest or jacket with them.

"I suppose you can't light a fire?" she said. "The firepit is outside the crime scene area and you guys look cold."

"We ran out of coffee," one admitted frankly.

His chest plate said his name was Carson. "We'll be relieved soon, though, Ranger. Only four hours at a stretch. If they need us up here tomorrow, we'll both be better prepared."

"You're not from around here, huh?" That seemed apparent. Anyone who lived in these parts knew how chilly it could get up here even at the height of summer.

"That's obvious, I guess," said the other guy. His last name was Bolling and his face was so fresh looking he could have passed for eighteen. Which she guessed was possible, however unlikely. "I'm from a small town in Nevada and I got sick of being hot."

Blaire had to laugh, and the two men joined her. She looked at Carson. "You, too?"

"Different town, more Midwestern. I wanted mountains. Visions of hiking and skiing. That kind of thing."

"I'll bet you never thought you'd be standing guard like this in the middle of nowhere."

"Not high on my list," Bolling said. "So is the skiing good?"

"We still don't have a downhill slope right around here. Something goes wrong with every attempt. But if you want to off-trail cross-country, that's great. So is snowshoeing. Just check in with me or with the national forest before you go. I need to know you're out here and you need to know if we have avalanche conditions. Mind if I walk around a bit?"

Carson chuckled. "I think you're in charge of this place except for the roped-off area."

"Yeah, that's yours."

She circled the campground, eyeing the signs of the hurried departures yesterday. And they had been hurried. Sure, it was unlikely the shooter was around or they'd have known it for certain, but she couldn't blame them for wanting to get the hell away from here.

Death had visited a few tents over. And it was not a natural death. Uneasiness would cause almost anyone to want to get as far away as possible.

She knew she and Gus had planned to check out the area together, but he also had responsibilities at the national forest. Her load was a lot lighter, for the most part. She could afford to set her staff to replacing fire rings, especially now that they were empty of campers.

She had no idea what she expected to find that the scene techs hadn't. They'd probably applied their version of a fine-tooth comb to most of the area, even beyond the circle of yellow tape.

But she kept walking slowly anyway. A campground was an unlikely place to pick up a trail, though. People were in constant motion at their sites and places in between. All of them had to traipse to one of the two outdoor chemical toilets, which meant they either walked around tents or passed between them. Kids, especially, scuffed the ground and kicked up needles and duff.

She paused at one spot where she had to smile. It seemed some kids had been laying out roads, probably to use to play with miniature cars. There were even a couple of twigs broken off trees and firmly planted to make the road look tree-lined. Clever.

How many kids had she seen last night? Not many, but that didn't mean they weren't there. Their parents might have insisted they stay inside tents.

Then she spied something red that was half-buried in earth and squatted. A small metal car, she realized as she brushed the debris away. She hoped it wasn't someone's favorite.

Just in case she got a letter in a week or so from some youngster, she slipped it into her vest pocket. It wouldn't be the first time she'd heard from a kid who'd left something behind and who couldn't come back to retrieve it. Usually it was an inexpensive, small item that the parents didn't consider worth the time and effort to return for. She could understand both sides of that issue, but she didn't mind sending a toy back if it made a boy or girl happy. In fact, just doing it always made her smile.

Since Afghanistan, her smiles had become rarer and far more precious to her when she could summon a genuine one. Gone were the days when laughter came easily. She hoped both would return eventually. She had to believe they would. A battlefield was a helluva place to lose all your illusions, and while humor had carried most of them through, it had become an increasingly dark humor. Something that no one on the outside would ever understand.

Swallowing her memories yet again, she forced herself to move slowly and sweep the ground with her eyes. The guy had to have come from somewhere. He wasn't a ghost.

There was a basic rule to investigation: whoever took something from a scene also left something behind. She'd first learned that in Afghanistan when they'd been tracking the people who had attacked them or one of their other convoys. Nobody could move over even the rockiest ground without leaving traces, however minor.

But this damn forest floor was a challenge unto itself. So much loose debris, easily scuffed and stirred. Even the wind could move it around. Moreover, under the trees it was soft, softer than a carpet, and footprints would disappear quickly unless boots scraped. Weight alone didn't make a lasting impression, not unless it rained, and rain here at this time of year was rare enough. They certainly hadn't had any in the several days leading up to the murder.

Eventually she called it a day. A wider perimeter would need the help that Gus promised and it might be a wild-goose chase anyway.

The killer was obviously skilled, had clearly taken great care not to leave a trail behind him.

Which left the question: Why Jasper? And why when his kid was there? Was Jimmy an unexpected complication for him? Too late to back out?

She seemed to remember one of the campers saying Jasper had brought his son up here just for the weekend. Yeah, if someone had been stalking him, Jimmy was probably a complete surprise.

She found herself once again hoping Jimmy could forget that night. If he retained any memory of it at all, she hoped it was of a space blanket and a ride in a police car. Not what had happened inside that tent.

Heading back, she passed the two cold deputies again. They no longer sat, but were moving from foot to foot. Too bad she hadn't picked up another survival blanket to offer them. "Much longer?" she asked.

Bolling looked at his watch. "A little less than an hour."

She nodded. "Keep warm." As if they could do much about it without lighting a small fire, which they didn't seem inclined to do. Maybe they didn't know how.

Shaking her head, knowing their relief was already on the way, she headed back to her truck, walking among the tall trees and the occasional brush that looked parched.

The peace she usually found in these woods had been shattered, she realized. The niggling uneasiness she'd been trying to ignore hit her full force during her walk back to her truck. A killer had stalked these woods. He might still be out there. He might be watching even now. And he could always return to repeat his crime.

She told herself not to be fanciful, but she'd spent time in a place where such threats were as real as the air she breathed and the ground she walked on.

The guy could be out there right now, savoring his kill, enjoying his apparent success, wanting to see everything that happened. Hadn't she read somewhere that criminals often came back to the scene, especially to watch the cops?

Or it could be another kind of killer. The kind who got a kick out of reliving his actions. Who enjoyed the sense of power the killing gave him. Or the secret power of being so close to the very cops who were supposed to find him. Cat and mouse, maybe.

His motivation scarcely mattered at this point, though it might become useful eventually. No, all that mattered right now was that these woods were haunted by the ghost of a dead man and the evil of a murderer. That a little boy's cries might have soaked into the very trees and earth, leaving a psychic stain.

God, was she losing it?

But her step quickened anyway. Back to HQ. Back to check on her team. To call the sheriff and ask if they'd learned anything at all.

Despite every effort to ignore the feeling, she paused and looked back twice. The sense of being watched persisted, even though she could detect nothing.

An icy trickle ran down her spine.

A THOUSAND YARDS away in a small hide left by some hunter in a past season, Will and Karl peered through high-powered binoculars. They'd happened on this point during reconnaissance during their spring planning and were delighted with it.

Here, below the tree line, there were few spots where one could see any great distance through the grid work of tree trunks and the laciness of tree branches. Not much brush under these trees, but not much open space for any appreciable distance.

This was a natural forest, not one neatly replanted by a lumber company, which would have given them corridors to peer along. No, here nature did her best to scatter the trees everywhere, giving each a better chance at a long life.

Some saplings added to the screening effect,

huddled around the base of mother trees that, science had learned, actually provided nutrients to their offspring. On occasion, an older tree would sacrifice its life to ensure the growth of the new ones. Roots underground were carriers of messages and food.

Will had read about it. It tickled him to think of how much a forest was invisibly intertwined. When he was in a fanciful mood, he'd sometimes close his eyes and imagine a brightly lit neural-type network running beneath his feet, messages passing among the sheltering trees.

Then there was that massive fungus scientists had discovered under the ground that turned out to be a single organism covering square miles. As he started thinking about that, however, Karl spoke, shattering the moment.

"Jeff did it."

Yes, he'd done it. The solitary tent surrounded by crime scene tape and the two deputies wandering around as if they wished they were anywhere else… It was all the diagram he needed. But he remained anyway, peering through the binoculars, both enjoying the success and wanting to annoy Karl, who felt no appreciation of the miracle under them, buried in the ground.

Once he'd tried to tell Karl about it. Once was enough. It didn't even matter to him that it was actual science. Not Karl. He prided himself on being hardheaded. Will could tell him about it, and Karl would absorb the information factually and move on, finding nothing entrancing about it.

That was the only thing he didn't like about Karl. Had never liked, even though they were good friends in every other way. Karl had a distinct lack of imagination. A trait that proved helpful in this endeavor, were Will to be honest about it.

While he himself might see a network of patterns and possibilities and race down various avenues of attack, Karl remained firmly grounded in their scouting expeditions and what they knew and didn't know. He wasn't one to make even a small assumption.

Although sending Jeff on this expedition had left them both wondering if he'd just walk into the nearest police station.

They had that covered. Two against one, if Jeff tried to nail them, the two of them would nail him. They were each the other's alibi.

Not that they'd need one. This was their fifth kill in the last two summers, and neither he nor Karl had ever left a shred of evidence. Hell, the murders hadn't even been linked to one another.

They'd vastly overshadowed careless Leopold and Loeb. Funny, though, Will thought while watching the campground, seeing the ranger stray around out farther looking for something.

He and Karl hadn't been content to prove the point and stop at one.

No. He and Karl had discovered a real taste for this kind of hunting. Deer could be slipperier, of course, but hunting a human? They weren't nearly as evasive, but they were so much more dangerous to take down.

It was always possible to leave traces, and cops would be looking, unlike when you took a deer during season with a license. They'd be paying attention to anything out of line. And if you weren't cautious enough, your victim might get wind that he was being stalked.

It wasn't the top thing on most people's minds, which had aided them, but one of their vics had had an almost preternatural sense that he was being followed. When they realized he seemed to be taking evasive action, they'd nearly salivated over the prospect of taking him out. A *real* challenge.

He studied the campground below once again, satisfying himself that no one seemed to be acting as if there was something significant to find.

Karl spoke, lowering his own binoculars. "Jeff's a wimp. I still can't believe he managed this."

"We kind of put him on the spot," Will reminded him.

Karl turned his head a bit to look at him. He shifted as if he were getting tired of lying on his stomach on the hard rock. "Would you have killed him?"

"I said I would."

"But he's one of us."

Will put down his own binoculars, lifting a brow. "He's one of us until he screws us. How far do you trust him?"

"More than I did a few days ago."

"Exactly. He's in it all the way now. But if he'd backed off, neither of us would have had a choice."

Karl nodded. "I know. I wish to hell he hadn't found out. Been jumpy since I learned he knew what we're doing. He's always been a bit of a coward. I like the guy, always have. We grew up together, went to college together. Joined the same fraternity, screwed the same girls…"

"Hey, that's almost as much of a crime these days as shooting someone."

Karl afforded one of his cold smiles. "Guess so, but I seem to remember those sorority gals fighting to get an invitation to our parties. And it wasn't a secret we were looking to get laid."

"Usually that was true. I remember a few who didn't seem to be clued in, though."

Karl nodded and lifted his binoculars again.

There *were* a few, Will recalled. Girls who were taken by surprise and had to be silenced before they got someone in trouble. Silencing them had been pathetically easy, though. All they'd had to do was tell them the stories they'd make up about the girls. How they'd come off looking like two-bit hookers. The strength of the fraternity, its numbers.

In a smaller way, he and Karl had that strength now, more so with Jeff actively involved.

God, how had that man pieced it all together from a few snips of conversation he'd overheard between Will and Karl? Why had he even believed it? What had been the clue that had made Jeff realize it was no longer a game?

Someday he was going to make Jeff spill the beans. But not yet. Jeff was entirely too nervous. He didn't want to do anything that might make Jeff take flight.

"I don't like that ranger," Karl remarked.

Will picked up his binoculars, focused them again and found the woman. "Why not?"

"She just picked up something from the ground and put it in her pocket. She's actively searching outside the crime scene area."

"She won't find anything useful," Will said, although sudden uncertainty made his stomach sink.

"She shouldn't if Jeff did what we said. But she just found something and picked it up. I couldn't tell what it was."

"Hell."

He zeroed in on the woman more closely, but she scanned the ground for a little while longer before waving to the deputies and heading for the parking lot. She didn't seem to be in a hurry, which could well be the best news for them.

At least until she started down the rutty walking path to the parking lot. Her step quickened, then quickened again and he saw her looking over her shoulder.

"What the hell?" he muttered.

She paused again and looked back.

"She senses we're watching," Karl said abruptly. "Look at something else."

"But…" Will started.

"No *buts*. If she'd found something she'd have showed it to the deputies. Instead she just stuck it in her pocket. Let it go."

Will, who'd been letting a lot go without much trouble for the last few years, suddenly found himself unable to do that. What had she picked up? It had been important enough to tuck in her pocket. Why hadn't she given it to the deputies?

Karl was probably right, he assured himself. But the way she'd looked back, twice… His stomach flipped again.

"Let it go," Karl said again. "People can often tell when they're being watched. It's some kind of instinct. But since she couldn't see anyone, she's probably convinced she imagined it."

"It would be easy enough," Will remarked. His literal-minded Karl might not get it, but Will himself had no desire to be any closer to that campsite. Something might be lurking down there, although he didn't want to put a name to it. He often told himself he didn't believe in ghosts or all that crap.

But the truth was, he feared they might exist.

That was one thing he hadn't considered when he'd embarked on this venture with his friends: that he might be collecting ghosts that could haunt him. Where was it written that they had to stay where they were killed?

He swore under his breath and rolled onto his back, looking up at the graying sky. "It's going to rain. Maybe we should go."

"It rarely rains up here."

"Don't you smell it?" He had to get out of here. Now. Because he honestly felt as if *something* were watching him.

"Well, we're supposed to meet Jeff at the lodge this evening," Karl said grudgingly. He pulled out a cigar from an inner pocket on his jacket. "Just a few puffs, first."

They were far enough away that the tobacco smell should waft away to the west, away from the campground and the deputies if it could even reach that far.

Giving in, Will pulled out a cigar of his own and clipped the end with his pocket tool before lighting it from a butane lighter. Then he held the flame to Karl, who did the same. The cellophane wrappers got shoved deep into their pockets.

It *was* relaxing, Will admitted to himself. Staring up at the graying sky that didn't look all that threatening yet. Lying still, refusing to think about all the worrisome problems that had been stalking *him* since they embarked on this venture.

Would he undo it? No way. He'd gotten thrills for a lifetime the last couple of years.

"What's eating you?" Karl asked after a few minutes. "You're edgy."

Well, there was no way Will would tell him that he didn't like being within range of the scenes where any of the victims had died. He stayed away once the deed was done. It was always Karl, whether it had been his kill or not, who wanted to go back and look the site over. Some quirk or odd fascination.

"Coming back could be dangerous," he said finally, although he didn't say how. No need for that.

"They would never look up here. You know that. We can look down on them, but when we checked it out two months ago, we realized this position was well shielded from below. Different sight lines. You know that. Besides, those deputies look bored out of their minds."

"Yeah." He puffed on his cigar, liking the way it tasted and gave him a mild buzz. "That ranger was acting weird."

"She probably just wants the campground back. Funny, though," Karl added.

"Yeah?"

"Every campground in the park emptied out. Talk about having an impact."

"Kind of a broad-brush response," Will agreed. That hadn't happened before. He pondered that reaction for the next ten minutes while drawing occasionally on his cigar. Maybe it was because this park was so small. While they'd chosen the most rustic of the campsites, farthest from the ranger's cabin and the entrance, the distance wasn't huge. If people thought a killer was hanging out in these woods, yeah, they'd get the hell out.

Abruptly, he returned to the moment as a huge drop of rain hit the tip of his nose. While he wandered in his thoughts, the sky had darkened considerably, and for the first time, he heard the rumble of thunder.

He spared a thought for those deputies standing guard below, not that he cared about them. The rain would mess up the scene even more, covering any inadvertent tracks Jeff might have left. Not that he thought any had been left. They'd picked a time when the campground would be full and well scuffed up by the campers. Probably covered with bits of their trash, as well.

He looked at his cigar, hating to put it out. He bought only expensive ones and felt guiltier about wasting them than he felt about wasting food.

He sat up and Karl did, too, after some raindrops splattered his face.

"We've seen enough for now," he told Karl.

"Yeah. Jeff did the job. If he followed all his instructions, we're clear."

Will looked at him. "Of course we're clear. Why wouldn't we be? He's been doing the stalking part with us since the beginning. He practiced the approaches. He's as good as either of us."

"Maybe."

Will sometimes thoroughly disliked Karl. Not for long, but there were moments. This was one of them. "No *maybe* about it," he said firmly.

The sky opened up, settling the question of what to do with the cigar as sheets of rain fell. He cussed, ground out his cigar and tossed the stogie to the ground, kicking leaves and pine needles over it. The rain would take care of it. Karl followed suit.

Together they rose, gave one last look back down the mountain, then started heading over the crest and back to their vehicle. Another successful hunt.

Irritated as he'd begun to feel, Will smiled as the rain hid them in its gray veils. Jeff had graduated. Maybe they ought to throw him a small party.

Chapter Five

Gus spent a lot of time thinking about Blaire the next two days. He'd hated leaving her at night, knowing she was going to be all alone in the park. But he didn't want to hover and make her feel that he was doubtful of her ability to care for herself.

Dang, those campers from the other campgrounds had bailed even before the cops had released the folks at the crime scene. Word had traveled on the wind, apparently, and nobody wanted to be camping out here when there'd been a murder.

An unusual murder. It wasn't as if Jasper had been killed by his wife after an argument, or as if he'd gotten into a fight with someone else at the campground.

No, to all appearances this shooter had been a stranger. That might change once the cops dug into Jasper's background more deeply, but the people at the surrounding campgrounds weren't going to take a chance that it wasn't a grudge killing.

Even a few of the national forest campgrounds had cleared out. The farther they were from the state park, the less likely people had been to leave, but there was still a marked quiet.

Weird, especially since people booked sites months in advance to make sure they'd have a place to pitch a tent or park an RV. Weirder still when you considered how hard it was to find a place to camp anymore. Gone were the days he remembered from childhood where you could drop in almost any place and find a site.

Anyway, once he got things sorted out with his staff, leaving Holly Booker in charge of the front office and the rest of his people out doing their regular jobs with guns on their hips and in their saddle holsters, he headed for Blaire's place again. The need to check on her had been growing more powerful all day.

Once upon a time being a ranger had been a relatively safe job. Well, except for problems with wildlife, of course. But that had changed over the last decade or so. Rangers were getting shot. Not many, but enough that anyone who worked in the forest needed to be alert to strange activity.

Now they'd had this killing, and he wasn't convinced the shooter had left the woods. What better place to hide out than in the huge forests on the side of the mountain? And what if he hadn't settled whatever problem had caused him to do this in the first place?

Lack of knowledge about the victim frustrated him, but since he wasn't a member of the sheriff's department he thought it very unlikely they'd give him any useful information. Investigations were always kept close to the vest, and for good reasons.

Reasons that didn't keep him from feeling frustrated nor ease his concern about what might be going on over in the state park. Most of his staff were certified as law officers for the US Forest Service and carried weapons. Things were different on the other side of the line. Blaire was the only park ranger over there who was an authorized law officer. The rest were civilian seasonal hires. Given this was Wyoming, he figured any of them could come armed to work, but he had no idea what training they might have.

He was confident of Blaire's training, especially with her Army background, but come sunset she'd be all alone in that deserted park. The last two nights hadn't worried him so much with cops crawling all over the crime scene, but tonight?

He was worried.

He'd gone on a few solo missions when he'd been in spec ops, but he always had backup at the other end of his radio: a helicopter that could swoop in quickly if he got in trouble. Only once had that failed him, and he'd had to travel for three days as surreptitiously as he possibly could before he got a radio connection and found a reasonably safe place for the chopper to come in. But there was only that once.

Blaire was over there with no one nearby. He was the closest thing to a backup she had, and training combined with the recent murder made him feel he could back her up a whole lot better over there.

Holly was happy to take over for him. She seemed to like the office work almost as much as she enjoyed taking small groups on tours of the wildflowers and wildlife. She said she just liked meeting the people, and she had a natural way of making everyone feel like a friend.

He kind of lacked that ability. Too much had closed up inside him over the years. Trust didn't come easily, and chitchat was largely beyond him. Holly had a gift, and he didn't mind taking advantage of it when she enjoyed it.

For himself, he preferred to be out in the woods riding Scrappy, occasionally stopping by campgrounds for a few words with people, and if he chatted much it was with hikers. Loners like himself.

Scrappy seemed in no particular hurry this evening. He ambled along and Gus swayed in his saddle, enjoying the soothing sound of creaking leather. During a number of missions in Afghanistan, he'd ridden horseback on saddles provided by the Army, but this was somehow different. Hell, he'd never be able to put his finger on the triggers that could send him into rage or cause him to get so lost in memory he didn't know where he was.

Edginess was a constant companion. He lived with it as he lived with bouts of anxiety. Mostly he controlled it. Sometimes he thought that Scrappy was his personal comfort animal.

They reached the end of the trail and Scrappy turned toward the ranger's cabin and Blaire without any direction from him. He guessed he was getting predictable.

Blaire was sitting on her porch step as the twilight began to deepen. She waved when she saw him and stood.

"Coffee?" she called.

"When have I ever said no?"

He swung down from the saddle as Blaire went inside, presumably to bring him some coffee. He'd just reached her step when she reemerged carrying two insulated mugs. Even in midsummer, when the sun disappeared behind the mountains, the thin air began to take on a noticeable chill. She was wearing a blue sweater and jeans, and he pulled a flannel shirt out of his saddlebag to wear.

Scrappy eyed him from the side with one warm brown eye, then began to explore his surroundings. He'd tossed the reins loosely over his neck so they didn't get caught on something. Probably wouldn't be long before he shook them off anyway.

Blaire sat, and he sat beside her, resting his elbows on his knees, taking care to keep space between them. He didn't ever want her to feel as if he were encroaching.

"You hear anything?" she asked.

"Not a peep. You?"

"Nada. I did wander around up there at the outer edge of the campground. I found where some kids had been making roads in the duff and picked up a miniature red car in case some-one calls me or writes about it."

"Really? For a miniature car?"

She looked at him, a crooked smile tipping her mouth. "You had a deprived childhood, Gus. Small things can be the most important stuff in the world to a kid. This is a little tow truck. Even has a hook on the boom."

He felt a smile grow on his own face. "Really cool, then."

"Clearly." She laughed quietly. "You know, this place is this deserted only at the height of winter. An awful lot of people have canceled res-ervations and most haven't even asked for their deposits back."

"Really? I know we're quiet, too, at least on your side of the forest, but I didn't check cancellations."

"Ah," she said. "Holly is taking over."

Something in the way she said that made him uncomfortable. He decided to take the possible bull by the potential horns. "*Not* because she's a woman. She happens to like it."

"Did I say anything?"

"Your voice was hinting."

She laughed, a delightful sound. Like him, she seemed to have trouble laughing at times, but when she relaxed enough he enjoyed hearing the sound emerge from her. He was glad the laughter hadn't been totally wiped out of her. Sometimes he wondered if *he* had much left.

He glanced up the road that led to the higher campgrounds, especially the one where the murder had happened. "It seems so out of the blue," he remarked.

"I know. Especially with the kid there. I keep wondering who would do a thing like that. Had the boy's presence been unexpected? Did the shooter even see Jimmy before he pulled the trigger?"

"Questions without answers right now," he remarked unhelpfully, then hated the way that sounded. "Sorry, I didn't mean anything by that." He took a long swallow of hot coffee.

"I didn't think you did. It's true, though. I have all these questions rolling around in my head, and the answers are beyond my knowing. I wonder if the sheriff will even share anything with us. Probably not."

"Not unless he thinks it would be useful, is my guess." Gus shifted, watching Scrappy knock the end of a branch with his nose, as if he found it entertaining to watch it bounce. It was probably easier to understand that horse's mind than the killer's mind.

After a few minutes, she spoke again. "One of my seasonals gave me chills earlier. Dave Carr. You've met him, I think?"

"Yeah, doesn't he lead backcountry ski expeditions in the winter?"

"That's him."

"So how'd he give you chills?" Turning until he leaned back against the porch stanchion, Gus sipped more coffee and waited to hear.

"Apparently there was a buzz going around town yesterday and early this morning. Some people are claiming there's a serial killer running around the mountains all the way up to Yellowstone and over to Idaho."

Gus stiffened. "Why in the hell?"

"Five murders in two years. Of course, that doesn't mean much. They were all in different places, and you can't even say all of them were killed in tents. They were all asleep when they got shot, but one guy was in the bed of his pickup, pulled over at a turnout on an access road up near Yellowstone. Sleeping, yeah, but out in plain sight." She shook her head a little. "From what Dave said, there's really nothing to link the killings."

"Other than that they all happened in the mountains and the victims were all sleeping."

"*Presumed* to be sleeping. That's talk. I'd have to ask Gage if he can check on the murders, and right now he's probably too busy to be worrying about what happened hundreds of miles away."

"True." He settled again but turned the idea around in his head. Linking murders was a chancy thing at best, especially if widely spread apart. The killer would have to leave some kind of "calling card." And if he had, wouldn't someone have picked up on it by now?

Blaire put her mug down on the porch, linked her hands as she leaned forward to rest her arms on her thighs and stared into the deepening night. "I was up at the scene. Oh, I already told you that. Sheesh, I'm losing my wits."

"I doubt it. Little car, roads in the duff."

She flashed a smile his way. "Yeah, and they were making little trees out of the ends of branches. I bet those kids were having a blast."

"I would have," he admitted. "I was really into making roads and hills to drive my cars and trucks over. My dad told me once I ought to get into model railroading, build my own scenery."

"Why didn't you?"

"I didn't have a place to do it, or the money,

even though I was working at a sandwich shop, and then the Army."

Her crooked smile returned. "The Army would do it."

"Didn't leave me a whole lot of time for anything else. So, you were up at the scene? Why do I feel you have more to say about that?"

"Probably because you're perceptive and I do. Yeah, I was up there yesterday, about midday. Two miserable deputies standing watch, neither of them prepared for how chilly it can get in the thin air up there. I felt sorry for them. Anyway, I felt as if I was being watched."

That definitely snagged his attention. He'd learned the hard way never to dismiss that feeling. "But you didn't see anyone?"

"Not a soul, other than the deputies. It felt as if the woods were still trying to get back to normal after all that happened. Not quite the same, if you know what I mean."

"Disturbed. Yeah. I've felt it."

"So anyway, maybe it was my own reaction to events and the feeling that some animals have moved away for a while. I couldn't blame them."

"Me neither." He drained his mug and was about to set it down when Blaire asked, "You want some more? I have to admit I'm feeling reluctant to go to sleep tonight."

He eyed her closely. "Did you sleep last night?"

"Mostly. I guess it hadn't sunk in yet. Tonight

it's sinking in." Rising, she took his mug and her own. "If you want to come inside?"

"I'm kind of enjoying the night. Unless you'd rather be indoors."

"Not especially."

He stared out into the woods, noting that Scrappy had wandered closer to the cabin again. The horse seemed calm and content, which was a good sign. Nothing going on out there to put him on edge.

Now he, himself, was a different story. Almost always on edge. He wished he could contain it some way so that he could help Blaire relax because despite her outward demeanor, he sensed she was wound up tight inside.

She returned with more coffee and the surprising addition of a small package of cinnamon rolls. "Sugar's good for whatever ails you."

He summoned a smile. "Until you're diabetic."

"I'm not. My kingdom for a chocolate bar. I'm a chocoholic."

"A common affliction." He opened the package of rolls, which sat on a silvery tray, and helped himself to one, waiting for the next development. Because there would be one. They'd spent enough time chatting over the last two years for him to have learned the rhythms of their revelations. She had more to say. She was troubled.

"There's something wrong with this situation," she said eventually.

"No kidding."

She shook her head a little. "I don't just mean the murder. But think about it. The shooter knew to walk up to a tent. I'm betting a specific tent. You?"

He thought about it. "There were plenty to choose from. Okay, let's assume he had a specific target in mind."

"But if it wasn't some guy he knew…" She paused. "Jimmy's presence is bothering me. A lot. If the shooter knew Jasper, he'd know about Jasper's kid. If he knew Jasper well, he'd probably know the guy liked to bring his kid camping with him. So… This is an awful place to take out a man you're mad at if you know he might have a child with him. It'd make more sense to get him near work or home."

"Maybe so." He was listening to her spin a theory and wouldn't interject anything unless he saw a glaring flaw. So far, he didn't. People who were mad at someone didn't usually follow them to an out-of-the-way campground to off them. Unnecessary effort, no special benefit. Bigger chance of getting caught, actually.

As if she were reading his thoughts, she said virtually the same thing. "You want to get rid of someone you hate, do it in a heavily populated area without witnesses. Not out here where you might stand out like a sore thumb. Someone's got to know the shooter was in this area, and I seriously doubt he's a local."

He made a sound of agreement.

"I'm not used to thinking this way," she said slowly. "If I go off the rails, let me know."

"Like I'm used to thinking this way?"

That drew a fleeting smile from her, but it didn't reach her eyes. Damn, he wanted to see her blue eyes smile again.

"Anyway," Gus continued, "what I'm getting at is that the victim may have been selected at random. And that our killer must have done some scouting beforehand. How else would he know how to get in and get out so quickly and easily? He couldn't have just been wandering in the woods in the middle of the night."

He was slipping into tactical ways of thinking, and wasn't at all certain that was the right direction to take with this. It wasn't a military operation. No reason to think the killer had been thinking of…

The thought halted midstream. His mind swerved onto a slightly different track without much of a hitch. "Planned operation," he said. He felt her gaze settle on him, almost as warm as a touch. Damn, he needed to ignore the attraction he felt for her. It wouldn't be good for either of them. Besides, right now it seemed to be important to her to puzzle out this murder. Like they had any real information.

"Planned operation?" she repeated.

"Yeah. It crossed my mind for some reason." The only reason possibly being that occasionally he was distractible. He never used to be that way, but since coming home for good, he had his moments of wandering. To escape unpleasant thoughts mostly, he imagined. "I'm starting to think tactically."

She turned toward him, attentive. "Yeah," she said quietly. Same wavelength.

"So, say this was planned. How long was Jasper at the campground?"

"Two and a half weeks. I checked."

"Long enough to figure out his habits, to get a sense of the area and people around him. Long enough to plan an approach and egress."

She nodded and turned more, pulling up one leg until it was folded sideways on the porch in front of her, half a cross-legged posture. Nodding again, she sipped her coffee, evidently thinking about what he'd said.

Which, frankly, sounded like a load of crap to him now that he'd said it out loud. Was he proposing some kind of mastermind killer? To what end? Even a soldier like him wouldn't be thinking of such things if he wanted to get rid of somebody. Hell no. Get 'em in a dark alley late at night, shiv 'em in the middle of a crowd... Escape routes were easier to come by than on a nearly unpopulated mountain. Any one of those campers might have responded immediately to the gunshot. No killer had any way to know no one would.

"Doesn't make sense," he said before she could raise a list of objections that would probably mirror his own. "No reason for anyone to treat the murder tactically. Habitual thinking on my part."

"But not necessarily wrong." She looked down into her mug, remaining quiet again.

He turned his head to find Scrappy meandering around the gravel parking lot at the edge of the woods. He loved that gelding. Probably the only living thing he allowed himself to love anymore.

"Love," he said, for no particular reason, "is a helluva scary proposition. Friendship, too, for that matter."

"Where'd that come from?"

He turned his head, meeting her eyes. "The horse, believe it or not. He's got a long life expectancy. Iraq and Afghanistan taught me to be stingy with my feelings."

"Yeah, it sure did." She closed her eyes briefly. "Maybe too stingy. I don't know. That little boy really upset me, his terror and knowing he is going to grow up without his father. But I've seen it before. Half the world seems to live in that condition."

He nodded. Nothing to say to that. It wasn't

only lost comrades who haunted his nightmares, though. Plenty of civilians did, too.

"Well," she said, "if you think there's any possibility that this guy was stalking the victim, then we owe it to ourselves and everyone else to take a look-see."

"For a distant sight line."

She nodded. "A place someone could watch from and not be noticed."

He looked up the mountain. "We'll have to cover a lot of territory." No denying it. Hundreds if not thousands of acres.

"Let's start with some parameters. How far out would the guy have to hide? Would he choose upslope or down? Whatever we decide, we can expand the area later if we need to."

"We could be wasting our time."

"It's better than doing nothing at all."

With that he felt complete agreement.

THEY'D THROWN A party for him. Even a bottle of champagne, decent champagne. Jeff felt pretty good and kept his lone slipup from Karl and Will. He figured that one shell casing couldn't give him away. Like he'd already thought, the heat of the exploding powder it had contained probably would have burned away any oils his fingers might have left behind. No reason to mention it.

At best they might find a partial, and fat lot of good it would do the cops even though he'd been fingerprinted when he joined the Army. A partial wouldn't create a match strong enough to stand up on its own. He knew because he'd looked it up.

But once they parted ways, he began to gnaw worriedly on the idea of that shell casing anyway. Useless, he kept telling himself, but part of him couldn't believe it.

So, without telling the others, he decided to go back and scout around a bit. If they hadn't found the casing, he'd remove it. Simple. Make sure there was nothing there. And he'd drive up just like any other tourist so there'd be no risk.

But that shell casing was haunting him, causing him so much anxiety that he was having trouble sleeping.

Worse, it was probably too soon to go back. He had to be sure the local authorities felt the site had nothing left to offer them, that they were totally ready to release it and forget about it.

And he'd need a cover story in case anyone wondered about him being up there. Time. He had to make himself wait a little longer.

He had a couple of weeks before he started teaching again. If he wanted to. He'd considered applying for a sabbatical for the fall term, and his department chair was agreeable, asking only that he give the department a couple of weeks warning so they could arrange for a stand-in.

But the idea of the sabbatical no longer enticed him. Sitting in his comfy little house on the edge of Laramie was proving to tax him psychologically.

Because of what they'd made him do. Because of what he'd done. Because the cries of a young child still echoed in the corridors of his mind.

Hell, if he were to be honest, the shell casing was the least of his worries. The biggest worry was how he would live with himself now. And an equally big worry was that they would insist he do this again. That they wouldn't buy that he now was so deeply involved he couldn't talk.

Damn, this was supposed to have been a *game*. Not real killings, merely the planning of them. How had Will and Karl moved past that? He'd never guessed they were so warped.

How could he have known them for so long and failed to realize they were probably both psychopaths? No real feeling for anyone else.

And how could they have known him for so long and not believe him when he said he'd never tell. Loyalty would have stopped him. But they didn't believe him, they didn't trust him, and that told him even more about them.

Friends? He'd have been better off with enemies.

Finally, anxiety pushed him to look up the state park's website. He needed to make a plan for going back there, maybe with a metal detector. After all, people still sometimes panned for gold in the streams in these mountains. It wouldn't be weird for someone to want to wander around with a metal detector hoping to find a nugget.

So he could get a metal detector and look around until he found the shell casing and then get the hell out. Easy plan. No reason to tell the others because he still didn't want them to know he'd left that casing behind.

Slow down, he told himself. *Take it easy.* Don't make a mistake that could get him into serious trouble.

He hadn't really looked at the park's website before. They'd taken a brief drive up the road to do recon and that didn't require a website. All he had needed to find was that rustic campground that vehicles couldn't. It had been easier than anticipated, too. GPS was a wonderful thing, as was a satellite receiver to track where he was. No need for a nearby cell repeater.

Thus he really didn't know anything about Twin Rocks Campground. The web page had the usual scenery pictures, one of an RV campsite, another of a rustic site and some general information for day hikes. Clearly nobody had spent a whole lot of time or money on this page.

He was about to move on to something else when he saw a name at the bottom of the page:

Blaire Afton, Chief Ranger.

Everything inside him felt as if it congealed.

He had seen her from a distance on their one recon, but had thought he was mistaken.

Blaire Afton. That couldn't be the Blaire Afton he'd met in the Army and asked to go out with him. She'd declined, then he'd been injured in that training accident and mustered out. Turning to her brief bio page, he looked at her photo. It was the same Blaire Afton.

He hadn't really known her.

But what if she remembered him? What if his name came up somehow and she recalled him, either from the Army or from him passing her on his way up the road?

Suddenly a partial fingerprint on a shell casing seemed like a bigger deal. If the cops mentioned that it seemed to belong to a Jeffery Walston, would she remember the name after all this time? What if she saw him at the park and remembered his face?

He closed his laptop swiftly as if it could hide him from danger. Bad. Bad indeed. He knew the ranger, however slightly. She might be able to identify him if they somehow came up with his name. But Jeffery Walston wasn't an unusual name. It could be lots of guys.

Unless she saw him at the campground running around with a metal detector. Unless she connected him to the location of the murder.

God, he'd better stay away from her. Far away.

But that shell casing was practically burning a hole in his mind.

If he'd had the guts, he might have killed himself right then. Instead he sat in a cold sweat and faced the fact that he'd probably have to fess up about the shell casing…and God knew what else.

He'd smoked, hadn't he? Thank heaven it had rained. He couldn't have left any DNA behind, could he? Surely that casing wouldn't still hold enough skin oil to identify him, either by partial print or DNA.

Surely.

But he stared blankly as his heart skipped beats, and he didn't believe it one bit. He'd broken the rule. He'd left enough behind to identify him.

God help him when the others found out.

Whatever the risk, he had to go back and make sure he found that casing and picked up any cigarette butts, rain or no rain.

And try to avoid Blaire Afton.

But he knew what the guys would tell him. He knew it with leaden certainty. Jeffery Walston might be a common name, but if Blaire Afton could link it to a face, well…

They'd tell him to kill her. To get rid of her so she couldn't identify him. Or they'd get rid of him. Squeezing his eyes closed, he faced what would happen if he ran into the ranger. He had to avoid her at all costs while cleaning up the evidence. If she saw him...

He quivered, thinking about having to kill another person, this time one he knew, however slightly.

God, he still couldn't believe the mess he'd gotten into, so innocently. Just playing a game with friends.

Until he learned the game was no game.

Terror grew in him like a tangled vine, reaching every cell in his body and mind. He had to go back and remove any evidence. No, he hadn't been able to go back for the casing while the cops were poring over the site, but they had to be gone by now. So he had to hunt for the casing and remove it if it was still there. Then he needed to go to the observation point and remove anything that remained of his presence there. Then he'd be safe. Even if Karl and Will got mad at him, he'd be safe, and so would they.

It didn't help that the kid had screamed and cried until he couldn't erase the sound from his own head. It chased him, the way fear was chasing him. He was well and truly stuck and he could see only one way out that didn't involve his dying.

He needed to calm down, think clearly, make sure he knew exactly what to do so he didn't make things worse. Reaching for a pill bottle in his pocket, he pulled out a small white pill. For anxiety. To find calm.

He had a lot of thinking to do.

his pocket, he pulled out a small white pill. For an instant. To calculate.

It was a lot of figuring to do.

Chapter Six

"I'm off the next two days," Gus said to Blaire two nights later. "I've got time to do some poking around if you can manage it."

She nodded. As the night thickened around them, the hoot of an owl filled the air. A lonely sound, although that wasn't why the owl hooted.

She murmured, "The owl calls my name."

"Don't say that," Gus said sharply. "I don't take those things lightly and you shouldn't, either. We've both seen how easily and senselessly death can come."

Little light reached them. The moon had shrunk until it was barely a sliver, and clouds kept scudding over it. Still, he thought he saw a hint of wryness in her expression.

"Superstitious much?" she asked with a lightness that surprised him, mainly because it meant her mood was improving. "I was thinking of the book."

"Oh." He'd reacted too quickly. "Some indigenous peoples consider the owl's hoot to be a bad omen. I was thinking of that."

"That's okay. And really, any of us who've gone where we've been probably pick up some superstitions. Heck, my mother even handed me a few when I was a kid. The *knock-on-wood* kind. And she hated it if anyone spilled salt."

He gave a brief laugh. "Yeah, I learned a few of those, too. You got any Irish in the family? My mom was Irish and I think she picked up a tote bag full of stuff like, *never leave an umbrella open upside down in the house.* More than once I saw her leap up, telling me not to do that."

"I never heard that one."

"It's a belief if the umbrella is open upside down it'll catch troubles for the house and family. There were others, but I left most of them behind." He paused. "Except this." Reaching inside his shirt, he pulled out a chain necklace. "My Saint Christopher medal. Apparently, he's not really a saint after all, but plenty of us still carry him around."

"Belief is what matters." She stood, stretching. "Are you heading back or do you want to use the couch? I think it's comfortable enough."

He rose, too. "That'd be great. Let me see to Scrappy and give Holly a call. And what about you? Can you get some time off tomorrow?"

"I can take two days whenever I want. Given that we're deserted right now, nobody really needs to be here. But Dave's my assistant. He'll stand in for me. I was thinking of going to town, too. I need some staples and a few fresh bits for my fridge."

INSIDE, BLAIRE SCANNED her small refrigerator in the back kitchen to see what else she might need to add to the list she'd been building since she last went grocery shopping. She didn't consume much herself, but she kept extra on hand for Dave, in case he worked late and for when he filled in for her on her days off.

Come winter she'd have to keep the fridge full to the brim because getting out of the park could sometimes be uncertain. Right now, however, when she was able to take a day or two every week, it wasn't as big a concern.

She called Dave on the radio, and he said he'd be glad to fill in for her tomorrow. *Good guy, Dave.*

Much as she tried to distract herself, however, her thoughts kept coming back to the murder. And to Gus. She'd learned to trust him over the two years since they'd met. They had a lot in common, of course, but it was more than that. At some point they'd crossed a bridge and for her part she knew she had shared memories with him that she would have found nearly impossible to share with anyone else.

Now, like her, he wanted to do some investigating up at the campground. Being in the Army had given them a very different mind-set in some ways, and when you looked at the murder as if it were a campaign, a mission, things popped to mind that might not if you thought of it as merely a random crime.

She was having trouble with the whole idea of random. Especially since Dave had told her that people were starting to talk about other murders, as well, and that they might be linked somehow.

Tomorrow she was going to make time to talk to the sheriff. She didn't know how much he'd tell her, but it was sure worth a try. She needed something, some kind of information to settle her about this ugly incident. She'd never be comfortable with the idea that that man had been murdered, never feel quite easy when she recalled little Jimmy's fear and sobbing, but she had a need to…

Well, pigeonhole, she guessed. Although that wasn't right, either. But even in war you had ways of dealing with matters so you could shove them in a mental rucksack out of the way.

This murder wasn't amenable to that because there were too damn many questions. War was itself an answer to a lot of things she'd had to deal with. Yeah, it was random, it was hideous, it was unthinkable. Life in a land of nightmares. But it had a name and a way to look at it.

Jasper's murder had nothing to define it except "murder."

So she needed a reason of almost any kind. An old enemy. Someone who bore a grudge. His wife's lover. Damn near anything would do because just *murder* wasn't enough for her.

She was pondering this newly discovered quirk in herself when the door opened and Gus entered, carrying his saddle with tack thrown over his shoulder. "Where can I set this?"

"Anywhere you want to."

For the first time she thought about his horse. "Is Scrappy going to be all right? I mean, I don't have a covered area for the corral here."

"I used some buckets from your lean-to. He's got food and water. And he's used to this." Gus lowered the saddle to the floor near the sidewall where there was some space. "I often go camping when I can get away, and he's happy to hang around and amuse himself, or just sleep."

"Oh." She felt oddly foolish. "I didn't know."

"Why should you? And, of course, being the nice person you are, you want to know he's okay."

She shook her head a little. "I think I care more about animals than people these days. Sorry, I was lost in thought. I just realized I have a driving need to make pigeonholes."

"Pigeonholes?"

"Yeah." She turned to go to the back and the kitchen. "Beer?"

"Thanks."

She retrieved two longnecks from the fridge and brought them out front. He accepted one bottle, then sat on the edge of the couch that filled one side of the public office space. Her living room, such as it was.

"I always liked this sofa," he remarked. "You lucked out. All I have are some institutional-type chairs."

"The last ranger left it. It doesn't suffer from overuse." She smiled. "In fact, you're the only person who uses it regularly."

"Yeah, I come visit a lot. Do you mind?"

"Of course not. If I did, I'd have told you a long time ago."

He twisted the top off his beer, flipped it into the wastebasket that sat in front of the long business desk that separated the public area from her office and raised it in salute. "Back to pigeon-holes."

She didn't answer immediately, but went instead to get the office chair from behind the long bar and bring it around. She sat on it facing him, as she had so many past evenings. "Maybe not pigeonholes," she said finally, then took a sip of her beer. Icy cold, her throat welcomed it. The air was so dry up here.

"Then what?"

"Maybe what I'm trying to say is that I need some context. This murder is so random."

"That it is." He leaned back, crossing his legs loosely at the ankles. "So what do you need to know?"

At that she had to laugh. "Motive. Identity. All that stuff nobody probably knows yet. Nice as that would be, I realize I won't be told until the case is closed. But I still need something. Who was the victim? What did he do? Why was he here with his son and not the rest of his family?"

"Did he have any enemies?" he added.

She nodded, feeling rueful. "Context. I guess I don't want to believe he was chosen randomly by someone with an itch to kill. That makes me crazy."

"It'd make anyone crazy. Anyone who cares, that is." He sighed and tipped his head back as he swallowed some more beer. "I guess we have to wait for our answers."

She leaned forward on her chair, cradling her frigid beer in both hands. "I need to deal with this. It's unreasonable to be uneasy simply because I don't have all the answers. I had few enough of them in Afghanistan."

"It wasn't answers we had over there. It was one big reason. If any of us had stopped to ask *why*, we might have had a bigger problem. But the reason was baked in from the moment we arrived. It was a war. This isn't a war. I don't blame you for being uneasy. Hell, the whole reason I rode over here tonight was because I couldn't stop feeling uneasy about you being alone over here. I'd have been over here last night but I know how damn independent you are."

"Gus…"

He held up a hand and she fell silent. "Let me finish. This is no criticism of you, or an expression of doubt in your abilities to look after yourself. No, I was uneasy because we've got a big question mark with a gun running around out there and that's a lot more difficult to protect yourself against than some known."

"Known? How so?"

"How many sandbag walls did you sit behind in Kandahar? How much armor did you wear every time you poked your nose out? Can we turn this cabin into a fortress? Not likely. It's a whole different situation, and being alone out here isn't the safest place to be, not until we can be sure the killer has moved on."

She nodded slowly, accepting his arguments. And though she could be fiercely independent and resented any implication that she was somehow less capable than a man, fact was, she was touched by his concern for her.

She stared down at her hands, cradling the beer she had hardly tasted, and remembered her early days here. She'd been on maybe her third or fourth night, feeling a mixture of pride at her recent promotion and a bit of discomfort about whether she was ready for the responsibility. Being alone out here, though, had always felt soothing. Comfortable. A long way away from ugly thoughts, pain and anguish.

Then Gus had come riding out of the spring mist that clung close to the ground that day. Wisps of it parted before him and Scrappy. Except for his green jacket, the brass badge and the Forest Service hat, she'd have wondered who the hell was riding in when the park hadn't officially opened for the season.

Iconic, she'd thought then. Even for a girl raised in the West, he looked iconic.

He'd raised a hand to wave, calling, "I'm Gus Maddox, the head ranger at the national forest next door." He and his horse had come closer. "You must be Blaire Afton?"

Thus had begun a relationship that had started as two strangers with similar jobs, then had been welded by sharing that they were both vets and sometimes had some difficulties dealing with the past. The revelations had come slowly, carefully. Trust was hard won in some areas. But now she trusted him completely.

In all that time, they had remained friends who treated each other as colleagues and occasionally as comrades. When they met up, either at one of their cabins or in town for coffee, they had the kinds of conversations she'd had with the guys in her unit in the Army.

As if there was a line that couldn't be crossed. Had they still been in the service, that line would definitely be there. But that was in the past, and now was now, and she felt ever increasing urges to know him in other ways.

A striking man, he'd have made almost any woman drool. She was a little astonished to realize she was getting to the drooling stage with him.

For some reason, the thought cheered her up, drawing her out of the uneasy darkness that had been haunting her since the murder. It was like a permission slip to get out of the serious stuff for a little while.

She looked at the bottle in her hand and noticed she'd hardly made a dent in that beer. Good. This was no alcohol-fueled mood.

Rising from her chair, she went to sit on the couch, not too close, but not exactly tucked into the far end, either. Even from more than a foot away, she could detect his aromas, wonderful aromas, the faint scent of man mixed with the outdoors, a bit of horse and a bit of beer. Very masculine.

Very sexy.

Oh, God, was she about to do something stupid? His gray eyes, eyes the color of a late afternoon storm rolling in over the mountains, had fixed on her and settled. It was a frank stare.

She was crossing the invisible line. He sensed it. All of a sudden she was nervous and afraid to move. She didn't want to make him uncomfortable. She didn't want to risk the precious friendship they'd built, and in her experience taking a relationship beyond that eventually led to a parting of ways.

And what if they *did* have sex? Would they become uncomfortable with one another afterward? It might prove to be a major sacrifice.

But his eyes held hers, drew her as if they were magnetic. "Blaire?"

Frank words emerged. There was little she hadn't told him about the bad things in the past, and dissembling with Gus seemed impossible now. "I'm telling myself not to go where I'm thinking about going."

That made him smile. Man, she loved the way the corners of his eyes crinkled when the smile reached them. "You are, huh? Afraid of repercussions?"

"Aren't there always repercussions?"

"Depends." Leaning to one side, he put his beer bottle on the battered end table. Then he took hers from her hands and put it beside his.

"You," he said, "are the most attractive woman I've known in a long time. Like you, I've been trying not to risk our friendship. But a lot of good things can begin between friends."

She nodded as her mouth went dry. A tremor passed through her.

"I get your reluctance. I share it. But I want you."

Oh, boy. Magic words. They lit her up like a thousand sparklers, tingling in every cell. She felt almost as if she couldn't catch her breath.

He reached out and took her hands. His touch was warm, his fingers and palms a bit calloused from hard work. He looked down at her smaller hands, then squeezed her fingers and drew her over until she sat beside him.

"I don't want to mess things up, either," he said. "But a hug ought to be safe, shouldn't it?"

He was quite a perceptive man, she thought as she nodded and let him gently pull her closer. He'd sensed what she was thinking and had turned out to be thinking along the same lines. As his arm wrapped around her, cuddling her to his side, she felt as if a spring-tight tension in her released. She relaxed, more completely than she had in a long time. She softened.

In the hollow of his shoulder, she found a firm pillow, and she could hear the beating of his heart, strong and steady. The arm he had wrapped around her gave her a gentle squeeze, then his hand began to stroke her arm.

Apparently trying to make sure matters didn't

progress further until and unless they were both ready, he began to talk about tomorrow. "Do you have good topographic maps for the area we're going to explore?"

"Yeah. Down to a meter or so. Some geology students did it as a class project a while back. There may be some differences, though. The mountain moves."

"That it does. Rocks fall, landslides happen... But whatever you have, let's mark out a plan of action tomorrow."

"Sounds good."

"But first you want to go to town, right?"

"I need a few things, but that could wait. What I really want is to talk to the sheriff."

"I've had cause to talk to Dalton quite a few times when we've had problems. He's a good man."

She nodded, loving the way the soft flannel of his shirt felt beneath her cheek. "He used to head up the crime scene unit before he was elected sheriff."

"And before that, undercover DEA." He gave a muted laugh. "That guy has a lot of experience under his belt. Even if he can't share details with us, maybe he can offer a few opinions or speculations."

"A sense of what might have been going on," she agreed. "He doesn't strike me as a man who likes the idea of a random killing, either."

"Stranger killings are the hardest to solve." A slight sigh escaped him. "More beer?"

"I misjudged my mood."

She felt, rather than saw, his nod, then his movements as he reached for his own bottle and took a few swallows. Tentatively she let her hand come to rest on one of his denim-clad thighs. She felt the muscles jump a bit at the touch, then relax. God, he was as hard as steel. Must be all that riding.

But he didn't reject her touch, nor did he do anything to encourage it. Her hand began to absorb his warmth, and she felt an even deeper relaxation filling her. Like a cat finding sunlight, she thought with some amusement at herself.

"I'm making too much of this," she remarked. "Too much. These things happen."

"Sure, they happen all the time in the desolate woods at a campground. If I thought you were making too much of this, I wouldn't have ridden over tonight. I'm concerned, too. You're right about needing a reason. Without it, we have no idea what this killer might be planning. Not a good time to be hanging out alone."

"But Jasper wasn't alone. He was in a campground with at least eight other camping groups. A really strange place to pull this."

"Which may be the biggest clue we have. Only problem is what to do with it."

Absently her fingers had begun to stroke the

taut denim on his thigh. She'd always loved the feel of worn denim, but it never occurred to her that she was self-comforting. Well, possibly in the depths of her mind, but she wasn't ready to face that.

Her self-image was one of toughness. She'd survived Afghanistan and all that went with that. She'd helped lead convoys through hell, and for all she was supposed to be a noncombatant, being female, she'd seen plenty of combat. She could handle a lot, and getting in a tizzy over a random murder struck her as an extreme overreaction.

Until she remembered Jimmy.

"It's the kid," she said presently, her voice evincing the slightest tremor. She hated the sound of weakness. "I should be able to just let this go, Gus. Let the sheriff handle it. But I can't and it's because of that little boy. Sure, maybe the guy had a ton of enemies. Maybe he was a drug dealer or a mob type, or whatever. But what kind of sick twist would have him shot when he was in a tent with his little boy?"

"That's troubling, isn't it?" Surprising her, he put his beer down then laid his hand over hers, clasping it lightly. "It bothers me, too. When it happened, I could see it might tear you apart."

"It was awful, Gus! That poor little kid! He didn't understand what had happened, thank God. And I'm fairly sure he didn't see how badly his father was wounded. I tried to keep my back to all that. But my God! What kind of sicko would do that?"

Gus didn't answer immediately. "Maybe he didn't know the child was there. But a sicko any way you look at it, kid or no kid. The man was sound asleep in a tent. No chance to defend himself."

"And no chance to protect Jimmy. That shooter could have hit the boy, too. Accidentally or not. Everything about it makes me furious."

"I feel pretty angry myself," he agreed.

But as her thoughts roamed even further backward in time, Blaire remembered her days in the Army. "Too many kids get traumatized," she said after a minute. "Too many. I just hope Jimmy has no clear memories of that night."

"Me, too." He squeezed her hand. "You did what you could to protect him, Blaire. You took good care of him, from what I could see."

"Little enough." She lowered her head, closing her eyes. "It's killing me," she admitted. "I want to get that guy. And I'm sure the impulse has mostly to do with Jimmy."

"Hardly surprising." He turned a little, drawing her into a closer embrace. "We can only do what we can," he reminded her. "Tomorrow we'll check with the sheriff to make sure we won't get in the way. Then we'll build our strategy."

"I don't recall any ops planning that happened

like this." Meaning the way he held her. She felt the laugh begin in his belly and roll upward until it emerged, a warm, amused sound.

"Nope," he agreed. "I remember always standing, or if we could sit, it was on miserable folding chairs around a table that was always gritty with dust. Hell, *we* were almost always gritty. We rigged a shower at our forward operating base and you'd barely switch into a clean set of camos before you'd be dusty again."

"It seemed like it. This is way more comfortable."

"By far."

She realized she was smiling into his shoulder. She wanted to wrap an arm around his waist but stopped herself. Lines that shouldn't be crossed. She never wanted to lose Gus's friendship.

She spoke. "I appreciate you not coming over last night to watch over me."

"I don't think I'm watching over you now. I've got a higher respect for your abilities, and it's not my place, anyway. I just kept getting this sense that it might be easier for you not to be alone at night."

"Given what happened, you're right." In Afghanistan she'd almost never been alone. That was the whole idea of a unit. But she didn't have a unit here to watch her back and there might still be a deranged killer out there running around in the woods. With everyone fleeing the camp-ground, that didn't leave many targets for him.

"This brings me back to the random thing," she remarked. "If he's still hanging around out there, looking for someone else to shoot, the target population just shrank to next to nothing."

"I thought about that," he agreed. "My end of the forest isn't quite as deserted as yours, but I'm not sure that should make me feel complacent."

"Then there's what Dave said this morning. People have started talking about scattered killings in the woods over the last few years. Some are calling for all of them to be investigated as one case."

"I'm sure Gage would do it if he had some proof."

"Exactly. When my computer is being reliable, I've spent hours today looking up news articles." She fell silent, wishing she could let go of all of it and just enjoy this rare opportunity to be so close to Gus.

"And?" he prompted her.

"I think I found the murders that concern some people." She sensed him grow more alert, a bit stiff.

"And?" he asked again.

"And people might be right. There are similarities but also differences."

"The gang-working-together idea?"

"Makes you wonder." Her heart grew heavy

at the thought. "Gang. It sounds so much worse in a way."

"Also maybe easier to solve. More people, more chances for a slipup."

She tilted her head and he obligingly tilted his so they could look at one another from a distance of about three inches.

"You're a glass-half-full kinda guy."

"I try. Wish I could say I always succeed."

She smiled, lifted her hand a bit and lightly touched his cheek. "You're a good influence."

"When I'm not in a dark pit." But he didn't seem to want to discuss that. "So, would it feel more like operational planning if I brought over a folding camp table and sprinkled a little dirt on it?"

The laugh escaped her. She hadn't even realized she was trembling on the cusp of one, but there it came. He had such a good effect on her, Gus did. He could steer a course through the difficult things and eventually bring back a happier mood. At least in her.

She was well aware he carried his own troubled memories, and he'd shared them with her. At least some of them. But like a cork, he always managed to bob back up. She could use a touch of that.

"Sure. I could even cut up the map."

He laughed again, his gray eyes dancing. "Absolutely. After all, every battle occurs at the juncture between four map sections…"

"In the dark and in the rain," she completed for him. An old saying, truer than she would have believed until she faced it.

"We do so much on computers now," she remarked, remembering scrolling through maps that were downloaded from a satellite.

"When the connection worked. I didn't like the limited view on the computer, though. Call me old-fashioned, but I always wanted a big paper map."

"Well, that's what I've got. Better yet, they're rolled, not folded, so no tears, and no corners at a point where we want to be."

He chuckled again. "There we go. I couldn't ask for better. Do you have any idea how the terrain may have changed since the mapping?"

"Some, but I've never done a complete survey. Basically, I'm here to make sure campers are safe and that no one commits vandalism or annoys anyone else. I know the ground I routinely cover pretty well. Then comes winter and it all changes anyway."

"Yeah. And we're out there with an eye on possible avalanche risks after a heavy snow." She knew he had pretty much the same winter tasks.

"I'm not exactly looking for boulders that might have moved a few feet." Closing a park didn't mean no one would use it. A surprising number of people showed up to cross-country ski on fresh unpacked snow, or to hike around on snowshoes. Hardy types, but they weren't always aware of winter dangers.

Yes, there was a sign out front, and in several other locations, warning people they entered at their own risk. But that didn't mean Blaire didn't keep an eye out. She lived here year-round, including the deep winter months, so if someone needed something and could get to her, they'd find help.

The hard part was keeping out the snowmobilers. The amount of damage they could do, even in the dead of winter, was appalling. It was a constant battle, even though there weren't that many places where the woods opened up to give them a path.

She closed her eyes, though, and thought about what it was like up here in the winter. Beautiful. Quiet. Serene. Almost magical. She found peace here. It filled her and mostly drove away the ghosts that followed her so restlessly.

"I wish it were winter," she heard herself murmur.

"Yeah. Me, too."

She realized he'd helped ease her tension to the point that she was getting sleepy. Much as she hated to do it, she eased away from him. "Let me get you some blankets."

"Tired?"

"I guess I've been more wound up since the murder than I realized."

He smiled and stood, offering his hand to help her up. "Sleep is always good. I think we both learned that the hard way. Where are the blankets? I can get them."

She pointed up to the loft. "My bedroom."

"Then just toss them down to me."

"Okay. You know where the half bath is?" Of course he did. This wasn't his first visit to this cabin. She must be even more worn out than she had thought.

After she tossed pillows and blankets down to him and said good-night, she pulled her boots off and flopped back on the bed. God, how had she grown so tired?

Then she faced it. She hadn't been sleeping well since the murder. She'd been on edge, wound up, and tossing and turning.

But right now, calm seemed to have descended. Gus was downstairs. She could let go of everything and let relaxation seep through her every cell.

Problems could wait for morning.

And almost before she finished the thought, she fell soundly asleep, still dressed, her legs hanging over the edge of the bed.

DOWNSTAIRS, GUS MADE his bed on the sofa, glad he'd decided to stay tonight. He got the feeling that Blaire seriously needed company. He could understand that.

Being locked inside your own head with your own worries and thoughts could be crazy-making. He'd been there and now tried to avoid it as much as possible.

Sometimes it was okay. Like her mentioning the winter woods. Like her, he loved that peaceful beauty. Or when he was out taking a lazy ride with Scrappy. But maybe being with Scrappy wasn't really being alone, he thought wryly.

He stepped outside to make sure his horse was okay and found that Scrappy had settled onto the ground, having evidently found himself a soft enough spot to curl up in. Scrappy plainly thought the world was safe tonight.

Back inside he reacquainted himself with the fact that a six-foot couch wasn't quite long enough for his six-foot-two length, but it wasn't impossible. Prop his head up a bit on the pillow and he just about made it.

Judging by the quiet from above, he guessed Blaire had fallen out quickly. Good. He suspected she might not have been sleeping well. Well, why should she? This murder had been bound to reawaken old wounds, even if only to a small degree. He felt some mental twinges himself. But like her, he wondered who could have committed an act like that.

A very sick man.

Which didn't comfort him even a little. It only made the perp more unpredictable.

Then, with nothing else he could do, he scooched onto his side and sought sleep. As with most soldiers, it wasn't hard to find.

Chapter Seven

Morning brought the dread visit to Jeff. The champagne they'd toasted him with the first night had worn off. Now they wanted to discuss their next move.

He wanted no part of it, and as they began to talk in the most general terms over coffee and sweet rolls, his mind ran around frantically trying to find a way to step out of this. To get away. To have no further part in their sick game.

Because he finally had to admit it wasn't just shocking, it was sick. He hardly recognized his friends anymore. They weren't the men he'd believed them to be.

Sociopaths. Psychopaths. Whatever. It didn't matter. They were strangers to him now, as if they'd been possessed by demons.

How could he get away from this? He couldn't commit another murder. He didn't want to know anything about what they intended to do next. No way.

But fear held him silent. Maybe too silent because Karl finally said to him, "What the hell is wrong with you, Jeff? You're as silent as a tomb."

That made Will laugh. Maybe in the past a phrase like that would have amused Jeff. Now it only made him feel ill.

Karl dropped his joking manner. "What's going on, Jeff?" This time it sounded like an inquisition, barely veiling a threat.

Jeff's mind, already skittering around like a cornered rat trying to find an escape, was now joined by a wildly hammering heart. He had to say something, preferably something that would get him out of this mess. He'd done his killing. They knew he couldn't squeal. He'd implicate himself as a murderer, not as an accomplice.

But what could he say that wouldn't make things worse?

He had to clear his throat to make sound emerge. "You didn't tell me there was a kid there."

"Kid?"

"Little one. In the tent with his father."

"Did he see you?" Will's immediate concern, Jeff thought bitterly. For his own safety.

"No. Too dark. Hell, I could barely see him. But I had to listen to his screams all the way up the mountain."

The two of them exchanged looks. Jeff was

rapidly reaching the point where he didn't care. If they killed him, at least he'd be out of this.

"We didn't know there was a kid," Karl said.

"Great planning," Jeff answered bitterly. "What if I'd hit him, too? You wanna talk about a manhunt?"

The other two were silent for a minute or so. Then Karl remarked, "They wouldn't be able to find us anyway. You didn't leave a trail."

Didn't leave a trail. Well, that was the big problem, wasn't it? A missing shell casing. And he was rapidly getting to the point where he didn't care if they knew.

"I left one thing," he blurted out.

Two heads swiveled to look at him, and neither looked very friendly. "What?" Karl demanded.

"A shell casing."

Will swore. "We warned you."

"Warn all you want. I forgot it. Do you know how many people were in that campground?" He was winding up now and didn't care where it took him. "Lots, and as soon as I fired my pistol, the kid started shrieking and the whole place woke up. I didn't have time to pull out my penlight and look for a casing. I had to get the hell out."

Although the truth of it was, he hadn't even remembered the casing. He might well have been able to find it and remove it. The chance the police hadn't found it was slim, but he was going to have to go back and look for it anyway, because he couldn't take the chance that he'd left evidence that could identify him and that it was still lying out there waiting to be found.

Bad enough he'd had to commit the murder. He sure as hell didn't want to *pay* for it.

"It's probably no big deal," Karl said a few minutes later. "The heat of the exploding powder probably would have burned it clean."

"And if it didn't?" Will demanded.

Karl shrugged. "Say it's got a fingerprint or two. Partials at best. And Jeff's never been fingerprinted, have you?"

Jeff couldn't force the lie past his throat. It was as if a vise clamped it and wouldn't let him speak.

"Jeff?" Will's voice had tightened and lowered until it almost sounded like a growled threat. "Fingerprints?"

Jeff wished he were already dead. He'd like to be out of body, watching this all from the ceiling. He wasn't going to get out of this, though. His silence was already an answer.

"When I enlisted in the Army. They took everyone's prints."

Karl swore and jumped up from his chair.

Will looked at him. "You said there'd be nothing left," Jeff said.

"There shouldn't be. That doesn't mean there won't be."

Jeff cringed instinctively as Will raised his hand. He expected to be struck, and having experienced that once before years ago, he knew it would be painful. The man was religious about staying in shape, and part of that was bodybuilding.

But Will didn't strike him. He lowered his hand and said, "We ought to bury you out back right now."

Jeff felt a flare of anger, a welcome relief from the terror he'd been living with. These men were supposed to be his friends? What alternate universe had he been living in?

He leaped up and glared at both of them. "I never wanted to do this, and you know it. I only killed that guy because you threatened to kill me if I didn't. I'm not happy about it. And if I made a freaking mistake, I'm the only one who'll go down for it, and you know it!"

"How are we supposed to know that?" Will asked.

"Simple, you jackass. No matter what I might tell the cops, you could tell them I'm nuts. There's nothing to implicate *you*. Why would I even bother? I told you months ago I'm not a rat."

"And we warned you about leaving behind any evidence," Karl growled. "Damn it, Jeff, are you missing some screws?"

"No." Jeff was getting fed up beyond containment. "You're clear. What do you care if I get picked up?"

"You need to go back and find it," Karl said. "Because the crime scene people might not have. You need to look for the shell casing, Jeff."

"How could they have missed it?"

"They're not big-city cops. A bunch of rubes. They'd miss their own noses if they didn't have mirrors."

"I can't go back there," Jeff said finally, and sagged into his chair.

"Why not?"

"Because the time we went on recon, I saw the ranger."

Will waved a hand. "Wait a minute. Why were you walking up the road? We told you to avoid that!"

"Remember, you took me on the recon. And the night of the killing, I came in from the back just like you said."

"Then why..." Karl trailed off as if he couldn't find words.

"It's simple," Jeff admitted. "I knew the ranger when we were in the Army. Just briefly. If she saw me when we drove up there, she never recognized me. As far as she was concerned, I was a total stranger."

Karl and Will exchanged long looks, then Karl said, "You're a jerk, Jeff. A total jerk. What if she remembered you afterward? What if she wonders what the hell you were doing there? You should have told us. We'd have found another place."

"I'm telling you…"

"You don't get to tell me anything. There's only one solution for this. You go back and kill her."

GUS AND BLAIRE decided to make a small social occasion out of the morning. Gus took Scrappy back to his corral just as the first morning light was dusting the eastern sky with pink. A half hour later, as the rim of the sun just started to lift above the mountains, he picked up Blaire in his green Forest Service truck. Some of the large tools rattled in the back but that was par.

She climbed in beside him, a smile on her face. For now they were out to banish the ugly things and reach for the good ones. One of the best was breakfast at Maude's diner. For a little while she could allow her concern about what had happened to that man, Jasper, and by extension his little boy, move into the background.

She used to be better at putting things aside. She'd quickly learned when she was overseas that you just couldn't let things weigh on you constantly or you'd wear yourself out, or worse, become useless. Compartmentalizing, she thought it was called. Well, for the duration of breakfast she was going to compartmentalize the murder.

Maybe in a way what made it so hard for her

was the protectiveness she felt for all the people camping in the park. As if she were their caretaker or something, which was ridiculous. Still, she handed out bandages, topical antiseptics, advice on a whole bunch of things, like starting a fire in a firepit, and even, at times, how to assemble a tent.

Mothering adults. Did she have an overinflated sense of her own importance? Or did inexperienced people just decide to go camping?

Only some of Maude's morning regulars had arrived at the café, so they had no trouble finding a seat. Blaire had loved Maude's—or the City Diner as it was properly named—since the first time she had visited it. It was vintage in every respect, right down to the matching tape covering cracks in the upholstery of chairs and booths. The tabletops, some kind of plastic laminate, had been wiped so many times that they showed white spots. And the aromas...ah, the aromas. At this hour, they were mostly of coffee and frying bacon or ham, and enough to create an appetite even on a full stomach.

Her stomach was far from full.

They both ordered omelets filled with cheese and ham. Blaire chose rye toast on the side, but Gus asked for a double helping of home fries with his meal. And, of course, coffee, but this time Blaire ordered one of the lattes Maude had started making a few years ago, from what she understood. One concession to modernity.

It would have been nice to get through the meal without a reminder, but an older man rose from a nearby table and came over to speak to them with little preamble.

"So what's with that murder? You got any leads yet?"

Blaire weighed a response. This would be a bad time to shoot from the hip. Gus was looking at her, probably deciding that since the murder had happened in *her* park, she should answer. "The police are looking into it. Right now, you probably know as much as I do."

The man nodded, rubbing his chin. Calloused skin rasped on beard stubble. "Folks are talking about some other murders, too. Been five of them in the mountains."

"I wouldn't know about them."

He shook his head. "I think people are inclined to make up stories because it's more interesting, if you know what I mean. Well, I thought maybe you could give me some ammo to stop some of that talk."

"Sorry, I know as much as you do."

He glanced at her name tag. "Thanks, Ranger Afton." Then he returned to his table.

"So much for forgetting for half an hour," she mumbled as she lifted the latte to her lips.

"I guess once you poked your nose out, someone was going to ask about it."

"He could have been a bigger nuisance," she admitted and pulled a smile from somewhere. "So much for our little social hour."

"We can try it again around a campfire tonight."

Her smile broadened. "I like the sound of that." And she did. It had been a while since she'd done that, and never with Gus. Sometimes she held campfires with storytelling for guests at the camp, especially when there were quite a few children of appropriate age.

She enjoyed those times, times when all the bad stuff at the back of her mind went into dark corners and stayed there.

After breakfast, they walked over to the sheriff's office. Blaire didn't spend a whole lot of time with the police, but she knew a few of the officers and greeted them. Gus seemed to know everyone there who was getting ready to go out on patrol or settling into a desk. He was, after all, law enforcement himself.

She still found it hard to get to know people. Brief conversations with campers, or informative campfires, were different somehow. Odd, but she hadn't always been that way. Something had happened to her in her time in the Army. It was almost as if she were afraid to commit any real emotion, as if she feared the person would just leave. As so many of her friends had during that year in the 'Stan.

She gave herself an internal shake, telling herself not to go there. It was over except inside her own head. Ghosts. Just ghosts.

Velma, the eternal dispatcher, waved them back to Gage's office with a cigarette in her hand. Over her head on the wall a huge no-smoking sign hung.

Blaire stifled a giggle.

"Skip the coffee," Gus whispered as they entered the back hallway. "Some of the deputies say it tastes like embalming fluid."

Another reason to laugh. Was she ready for that? She guessed she was. But everything changed the instant they stepped into Gage Dalton's office.

The sheriff, one side of his face scarred by an old burn, motioned them to sit in the chairs facing his desk. If she sat just right, Blaire could see around the tippy stacks of paper and the old-fashioned cathode-ray tube monitor on the computer. That thing needed to be put out to pasture, she thought.

"Need a bigger desk?" she heard herself ask.

Gage chuckled. "I need not to have to keep every report on paper as well as on the computer. Don't ask me why. I keep thinking I should make an executive decision to put a halt to the duplication, but then a clerk over at the courthouse reminds me we'll always need a paper trail. What if the computers go down or get hacked? I still need an answer for that one. So, what's up?"

Gus looked at Blaire, so she spoke first. "We want to do a perimeter check, but we don't want to get in your way. And if there's anything you've discovered about the murder that you can share, it'd be really helpful."

Gage looked at both of them. "Don't you have your own park to watch?" he asked Gus.

"Right now I want to help catch this guy so Blaire isn't out there all alone at night wondering if he's still in the woods."

Gage nodded. "I hadn't thought of that. We've been presuming he's long gone. No reason to hang around. And as near as we can tell so far, he picked Jasper at random. He worked as an accountant for an oil company. No reason to have any enemies. God-fearing, churchgoing and nobody so far has a harsh word to say. Although that could change."

She couldn't help herself. "How is Jimmy? The little boy?"

"His mom says he doesn't seem to be aware of what happened, but she's taking him to therapy anyway. He's going to need help, at the very least, with dealing with his dad being gone for good."

"I should say so." She shook her head, remembering that sobbing little boy in her arms on a cold, cold night.

"His mom says she can't separate him from the rescue blanket, so you made a hit with that one."

"Space blanket," she said. "That's what I told him. Maybe he'll dream of being an astronaut." She sighed. "But back to the big questions. I'm hearing from one of my team members that people are talking about this murder being related to others."

"I'm hearing that, too. I have some investigators looking into it and consulting with other police departments. We'll see if we can find any links. God knows we need something more than a spent shell casing."

Gus leaned forward. "He left a shell casing behind? That's amateurish."

"Yeah, it is," Gage agreed. "Very. So the likelihood that he's responsible for other murders that left no evidence behind is pretty slim."

"Blaire had an idea," Gus said. He looked at her.

"It's probably silly," she said, ready to dismiss it.

"Nothing's silly," Gus replied, "and certainly not from you with where you've been. Spit it out."

She shrugged one shoulder. "It seems random. But when you add in the other murders people have mentioned, maybe… Maybe it's not one guy acting alone. Especially since I'm hearing that they're all different, but you say they left no evidence behind."

Gage nodded thoughtfully. "I'm not ready to agree, but it's an interesting notion. Let me see what I get back from other agencies. Then there's the question of what you mean by a perimeter search."

Gus spoke. "We were talking about how this guy had to have somewhere to watch the campground. To make sure when it was safe to go in, to choose his target, whatever. A staging location. We thought we might find something."

"Point is," Blaire admitted almost ruefully, "I'm not good at sitting on my hands. This might turn up evidence."

"You're thinking in bigger terms," Gage remarked. "Tactical terms."

Blaire nodded. "It's our training."

"It's good training. It's also a great idea. The likelihood that he just hung around until everyone went to sleep bugs me. But with kids running around the place, he'd probably be seen."

"Probably," they agreed as one.

"Go for it. At this point the likelihood we'll get anything useful off that shell casing is slim. I'll be able to match it to a weapon if we ever find it, but right now…" Gage shook his head. "Find me a pistol while you're at it."

A few minutes later, they were heading out with Gage's promise to share any information he received on the other murders. Not this investigation, of course. He couldn't breach that confidentiality. But the others? Most were probably cold cases by now. Few secrets he couldn't share.

Before they got out the door, however, Connie Parish and Beau Beauregard, both deputies, suggested coffee at Maude's. Blaire exchanged looks with Gus and got the impression that he felt that might be significant. He nodded to her and she smiled.

"Sure," she said.

Maude's had quieted some after the breakfast hour, and they had no trouble finding a relatively private booth. Coffee arrived automatically, and it seemed Maude had decided Blaire was a latte drinker, because that's what she received in a tall cup. Not that she was about to complain.

"Primarily," Connie said, speaking first, "I'm worried about you being out at the campground all alone, Blaire, especially at night. So is Beau. This was such a random killing, and the guy could still be out there. Wouldn't be the first weirdo we've had playing hermit in those mountains."

"Nor the last," Beau remarked. "The *he always kept to himself* kind don't always limit that to the apartment next door."

Despite herself, Blaire was amused. "What do you think we're dealing with here?"

"Damned if I know. The vic was an accountant. For an oil company," Connie said. "Now, how likely is that to get you shot on a camping trip? Oh, I suppose there could be reasons, but I can't imagine any. If he'd angered someone at the company, why follow him out here? This feels so random."

"At least it appears to be," Gus agreed. "But if you really think about it, a lot of life is random. Even so, maybe he had some debts he couldn't meet. Gambling, drugs."

"That's so cliché," Blaire murmured, unexpectedly drawing a laugh from the other three. "Well, it is," she protested. "Easy fallback position. Blame it on the vic."

He shrugged. "You're right. But we have so little to go on, at least as far as I know."

Turning her latte in her hands, Blaire studied it as if it might have answers. Afghanistan had been nothing like this, she thought. Nothing. It struck her as odd that one murder was bothering her so much after all that she'd lived through. Yet somehow this one murder seemed scarier. Maybe because it was so far inexplicable.

Beau spoke. "We were thinking we'd feel better if you had a dog, Blaire."

Her head snapped up. "A dog?"

"A trained police dog," Beau clarified. "I

spoke to Cadell Marcus yesterday. I don't know if you've met him, but he trains our K-9s. He's got a Malinois almost ready to go, and he said he'd be willing to pass her to you, or just let you keep her for a while, whichever you prefer."

This was so unexpected, Blaire had to think about it. She liked dogs. Hell, they'd had a few bomb sniffers with them in Afghanistan. She felt great respect for a dog's abilities. But she'd never thought of wanting or needing her own K-9.

"That isn't extreme?" she said finally.

"Hardly," Gus said drily. "I slept on your sofa last night because I didn't like the idea of you being alone out there. I know you can take care of yourself, but that didn't keep me from worrying one bit. Some things seem to be engraved on my DNA."

She might have laughed except right now she felt far from laughter. A man was dead, they didn't know why and some creep might be haunting the woods.

Before she could make up her mind, Gus spoke. "I was also thinking about getting her a horse. At least for now. We want to ride around up there looking for evidence of a staging area or an isolated camp. Gideon Ironheart's the man for that, right?"

Connie nodded. "My uncle-in-law," she explained to Blaire. "In case you don't know."

"I thought everyone in the county knew how

all the Parishes are related," Gus said. "It's one of the first things I heard about."

Connie flashed a grin. "For a while we just kept expanding. Anyway, if you want, I'll call Gideon. I'm sure he'll be glad to bring a mount to the park for Blaire. How well do you ride?"

"I'm pretty much a novice," Blaire warned her, but she had to admit she liked the idea of being able to ride around the mountain instead of hiking for a few days while they hunted for any kind of evidence. "I did some riding while I was in Afghanistan but I haven't done much since."

"Gideon will have a gentle, patient horse. He'll take care of everything."

"And the dog?" Beau prompted.

Blaire had to hesitate. Much as she liked dogs, she wasn't sure she wanted one living with her. She'd become attached, for one thing. For another, animals weren't allowed in the park. "You know we don't allow pets in the park. Mainly because people don't keep them leashed. They chase deer and other animals. Then, most people don't scoop up after them. So how can I have a dog and tell campers they can't?"

"Get him a K-9 vest," Beau said. "That should do all your explaining for you."

He had a point, but she still hesitated. "Let me think about it," she said finally. "Right now the place is completely empty, but give it a few days. Fears will subside and there'll be plenty of people around. Then none of you will have to worry about me being alone."

She was touched by their concern. Inwardly she was aware of her own uneasiness because of the incomprehensibility of this murder, but she didn't want to display it. She'd been to war. If she could survive that, even with some emotional damage, she could certainly survive this. And she had a reasonable, tested belief in her ability to look out for herself. Not that she was a super-hero or anything, but she could handle quite a bit.

Everything except someone creeping up on her in her sleep. But she had locks and a sturdy building. She wasn't sleeping in a tent like Jasper.

But something else was going on with the idea of getting a dog. "We had bomb-sniffing dogs in Afghanistan."

"Yup," Gus agreed, then waited.

"We lost a few." She closed her eyes. "Getting attached... I'm not ready to do that again, okay?"

"Okay," said Connie. "Let me call Gideon. We'll get you a horse on loan so you can roam around with Gus and check out the area faster. I bet he can get one up there by late this afternoon. Will you be around?"

Gus spoke. "It's my understanding that Blaire wants to lay in some supplies. Then?"

The question was directed at her. "Just some supplies. Gage said he'll let us know what he learns. Beyond that, I have no business." She turned her head toward Gus. "You?"

"The same." He looked at Connie and Beau. "Figure we'll be back in place at the park by two or a little after."

Connie nodded. "I'll call Gideon now."

THE TRIP TO the grocery felt almost like emerging from night into day. It was so damn normal, she thought as she and Gus wended their way through the aisles, sharing a cart. She even decided to splurge a little on a box of frozen clam strips and a bag of frozen North Atlantic cod. Her freezer wasn't large, so she had to resist a whole lot more than that and stick to staples like boneless, skinless chicken breasts that provided a good protein base for almost anything, some frozen veggies and canned goods that would keep for a while.

When she was done, she realized she'd bought more than she usually did, and looked at the sacks she piled into the back of Gus's truck.

"I overdid it," she remarked.

He laughed. "You, too?"

She shook her head a little. "I share with my staff once in a while, but you can't eat everything out of a box or a can. It gets boring."

"Jars," he said. "I depend on jars. Tomato sauce, Alfredo sauce, things like that."

She nodded. "I'm stocked with enough soup cans to feed an army, I believe."

"I love soup."

They were both pretty cheerful as they pulled out of town and began rolling toward the mountains and the park.

Gus brought up the problem of storage. It seemed a safe enough topic, she supposed, because with each passing mile the shadow of the murder seemed to be looming larger.

"Can't you get the state to give you a bigger refrigerator and freezer? It seems awfully small if you can't get out of the park for some reason."

"Mostly I only have to worry about myself," she answered. "I always have some backup in the cupboards during the summer, and come winter I've got the world's biggest freezer."

He laughed. "True that."

The road into the park began to rise before them, and way up above the mountain peak storm clouds seemed to be brewing. But something else was brewing inside Blaire, and finally she decided to address it directly.

"I must be crazy."

"Why?" He turned the wheel a bit trying to avoid a pothole. The truck bumped only a little.

"Because it's ridiculous to think the murderer might still be up there hiding out in the woods. And that even if he is, that he might kill someone else."

"I don't think that's crazy." Surprising her, he freed one hand from the wheel to reach over and squeeze hers. Just a quick squeeze because as the road grew rougher, he needed both hands to control the truck. "It would be easier to dismiss the idea if we knew why Jasper was killed. A reason for it. But as it stands, the whole damn thing is an ugly mystery, and now the possibility that five other murders might be linked makes it even worse."

"Serial killer," she said. The truck engine strained a little as the climb became steeper. A short distance with a steep grade that the park system kept talking about leveling out.

"Well, we don't know that, either. But as long as it's a possibility, there's no reason to feel crazy for worrying."

"I guess not. I didn't used to be so easy to creep out."

He snorted. "You're not used to this situation. Overseas we knew we were always at risk and the threat could come from anywhere. Here, we don't expect those things. It's so out of place in the park that it's downright jarring."

"So is this road," she remarked, trying to change the subject. She didn't want to give in to the morbid maundering of her imagination, especially since her experience in Afghanistan had given her enough vivid images and memories to fill in the imaginings. The important thing was to keep control of her mind.

Yeah. She'd been working on that for years. It ought to be a perfected skill by now, but occasionally the wrong stuff still popped up and disturbed her.

"We've been talking about resurfacing this road," she remarked as the truck jolted yet again. "I don't think we're high on the state's priority list, though. We're a small campground, comparatively speaking."

"With the national forest right next door, what do you expect?" he asked lightly. "We get the roads. If people want to drive a huge RV in, they come to us. On the other hand, your campgrounds offer a lot more privacy."

"Yeah. We get a lot of tent campers. Pop-up trailer types. Not so many big RVs, but quite a few smaller ones at lower altitudes where we have hookups."

Covering familiar ground, talking about stuff he already knew, probably because she was trying to cover up her crawling sense of unease. Like when she'd been on missions. Knowing the enemy was out there, never knowing when he might strike.

"You looking forward to having a horse for a few days?" he asked, bringing them around a hairpin bend where the road went from pavement to gravel.

"Yeah, except it occurred to me, too late, I know next to nothing about caring for one. Heck, those saddles we used in Afghanistan were nothing like the one you have."

"Well, I'll share a secret with you."

"What's that?"

He flashed a smile her way. "I'll help you take care of the horse. In fact, I'll bring Scrappy over and the two can share your corral for a few days. Make a party of it."

Her discomfort subsided a bit. "A party? Seriously? When we're looking for evidence to lead us to a killer?"

He laughed. "Thought you'd like that one."

At last they pulled through the official entrance to the campground and into the small parking lot in front of her cabin. Dave was sitting on the front porch on a battered lawn chair with his feet on the railing. He waved as they pulled up. A man of about forty, mostly bald, with a friendly face and a personal uniform of plaid shirts and jeans, he made people feel welcome. Blaire sometimes wondered if *she* did.

"Didn't expect you back so soon," Dave remarked. "I thought when you said you wanted a couple of days you planned to be scarce around here."

Blaire smiled. "I do. Someone's lending me a horse and Gus and I are going to take some rides in the mountains." Why did she feel as if she couldn't share the truth with Dave? He wasn't one for gossip, and what did it matter anyway? It wasn't as if she were embarking on a top secret mission where a little talk could cost lives.

She was slipping back into the military mindset. Whether that was good or bad, it was too soon to say. She guessed she'd find out.

"So you want me to hang around?" Dave asked. "Or come back tomorrow? I don't see two horses and it's getting kind of late in the day to take much of a ride anyway."

Blaire chewed her lip momentarily. "Would filling in for me tomorrow be a problem?"

"I'd planned to anyway. And an extra day if you want. My wife and kids went to Buffalo to visit her family, so it's not like anyone's going to miss me."

Gus spoke. "I need to go over to my place to get my horse and some supplies. If you could hang out here, I'll take Blaire with me and she can drive my truck back over while I bring Scrappy." He eyed Blaire. "If that's okay with you?"

"That's fine," she agreed. She liked the idea that Gus was evidently planning to stay another night, and that he'd help her learn how to take care of the horse that Gideon should be bringing.

"Just one thing," Gus said. "Gideon Ironheart is bringing a horse for Blaire to ride for a few days, so if it arrives while we're gone?"

Dave nodded. "That I can handle. The corral out back is still good, mainly because I fixed it up last spring. You never know when the state might decide it would help to get us mounts. On the other hand, the way the road paving argument is going, I figure I'll be walking or using the ATVs for years to come."

"They work," Blaire pointed out with humor.

"Sure, but they don't go everywhere a horse could."

She half smiled. "And they tear up the terrain."

"Exactly." Dave pretended to be struck by the thought. "I never thought of that. Sheesh, Blaire, you ought to pass that along to the powers that be. Hey, guys, the ATVs damage the environment."

"Probably no more than the campers," she retorted. "Okay, that's how we'll do it, then." She looked at Gus. "How long should we be?"

"An hour at most. By truck my cabin isn't that far away if you take the wood trail."

She knew what he meant. There was a road between the two cabins, basically two ruts that ran between the trees, but it shaved off a lot of travel time. Gus's truck had high suspension for dealing with the rugged terrain around the forest. It could probably handle it better than most ATVs.

Thanking Dave yet again, she climbed back into the truck with Gus, and they headed along the wood trail toward his headquarters.

Chapter Eight

Gus loaded the back of his truck with all kinds of horse needs, like bags of feed, currycombs and so on. He believed in taking care of any animal in his care, and some that simply needed help. When it came to Scrappy, however, it felt as if he were taking care of family.

Instead of taking the trail back to Blaire's place, he took the wood road. He led the way on Scrappy with her following behind in his truck. The day was beginning to wane. The sun had disappeared behind the mountain he was traveling over, and the light had become flat. It was still daytime, the sky above a brilliant blue, but the shadows beneath the trees seemed to have deepened anyway.

The forest didn't feel right, he thought. He supposed that was something left over from the war, but it was a feeling he couldn't dismiss anyway. As if a threat could lurk behind any tree.

Maybe it could. Some lunatic had killed a

man inoffensively sleeping in his tent. Killed him with his young son beside him. What kind of person did that? The question had been bugging him since the outset.

The kind of person who would do that was exactly the reason he couldn't bring himself to leave Blaire alone again. He'd fought his instincts the first nights after the murder, but finally he couldn't continue an internal war that clearly wasn't going to sign a cease-fire.

He was worried for Blaire. She was out there alone at night, and if the campground had been full to the rafters, he'd have felt he was extraneous. But everyone had fled after the murder, and there was still no sign of a return.

People had become spooked. Unless they caught the bad guy, Blaire's campground might remain mostly empty for the rest of the season. That meant she'd be all alone out there in the woods at night after her seasonal staff went home for the day. Ordinarily that wasn't something she, or he, would worry about.

Now he was worrying. The woods didn't feel right, and instinct was crawling up and down his spine telling him this wasn't over. How he could be sure of that, he didn't know, but he remained on high alert for anything that didn't seem normal. Anything that might indicate an important change of some kind.

For certain, he was in agreement with Blaire

that something about the murder seemed more like a planned operation. An assassination. Which made him truly eager to learn anything he could about the victim, but no one was going to feed that information to him. Police stuff. Civilians not wanted.

Yeah, he was a law enforcement officer, but only in the national forest. If the murder had happened over there, he'd be part of the investigation. This was different. He didn't have a clear idea of Blaire's role vis-à-vis this kind of thing. But wasn't she, too, law enforcement in the park? But maybe not for major crimes. Maybe she was expected to rely on local authorities. It wasn't as if she had the manpower to do much else.

But still… Maybe she could press Gage a little more. Maybe, given her position, he might be willing to share more with her than information about the other murders that were now worrying people.

And man, hadn't that seemed to come out of nowhere? All of a sudden people worrying about other murders that had happened in the woods over the last couple of years. Linked? How likely was that? He had no idea.

He just knew that his gut was screaming this wasn't over, and he couldn't stop worrying about Blaire.

Tomorrow they'd pack up some supplies and do a survey of the surrounding area. The killing had been planned. Of that he was certain. And that meant someone had spent at least a little time surveying the campground and the victim. Which also meant a greater likelihood the guy had left some kind of evidence behind.

He just hoped his need to protect Blaire wasn't offending her. She had experience in combat, in military operations, and while she hadn't been in special ops the way he had, it remained she was no greenhorn. He'd often felt kinship with the way her mind worked.

So maybe he should ask her if she resented his hovering. He couldn't blame her if she did. Yeah, he should ask. He should do her that courtesy.

He also needed to be wary of his attraction to her. He'd felt it when they first met, and it hadn't lessened any with time, but he honestly still didn't feel emotionally fit to engage in a meaningful relationship deeper than friendship. And from things she'd said occasionally, he believed she felt much the same way: wary.

A misstep could kill their friendship, and he treasured that too much to risk it. Still, sometimes his body ached with yearning when he thought of her or was around her.

Careful, dude. Just be careful.

The radio on his hip crackled and he lifted it to his ear. A satellite transceiver, it usually worked, but occasionally dense woods could interfere a bit. No real interference right now, though.

"Maddox," he said into the receiver.

"Hey, boss," came the voice of Tony Eschevarria.

"What's up?" Gus asked.

"You said you'd be out of pocket the next two days?"

"At least. Over at the state campground."

"Weird, that killing," Tony remarked, his voice crackling a bit. "Listen, a deputy is here. He's looking for you and I can send him over that way if you want."

"Sure thing. I should be there in about twenty minutes."

"I hope he's got good news, Gus."

"Me, too," Gus answered. "Me, too."

He clipped the brick back in its belt holder, then leaned forward to pat Scrappy's neck. The saddle creaked a bit, a sound he'd always loved, and nearly vanished in the shivering of deciduous tree leaves in the gentle breeze. The storm that had appeared to be building over the mountains hadn't materialized, but he swore he could smell it. Tonight, maybe.

The wood road, as they called it, little more than a cart track, had once been used by lumbers gathering wood to build the old mining town on Thunder Mountain, abandoned more than a century ago. Still, the cart tracks had been convenient enough that they'd been kept clear by usage over those years.

At last the track emerged onto a portion of paved roadway just above Blaire's cabin. A truck and horse trailer now filled part of the gravel lot, and Dave was standing out front talking to Gideon Ironheart. Gus smiled. He'd always liked Gideon.

The man had once been an ironworker who'd walked the high beams, but when he came here to visit his estranged brother, Micah Parish, he'd fallen in love with one of Micah's colleagues in the sheriff's office. At least that was the story. Anyway, these days Gideon raised horses, trained them for their owners and rescued mustangs. His two teenage children often led trail rides for tourists, sometimes at the national forest.

While Blaire parked the truck, he dismounted Scrappy and called a greeting to Gideon, who walked over with an extended hand. "I hear you're planning to do a little exploring with Blaire Afton."

"That's the plan. Thanks for the help."

Gideon grinned. "It's good for the horses to have a little adventure every now and then. I might have some big paddocks but they offer little new to explore. Lita will enjoy herself a whole bunch."

"Lita's the horse?" He heard Blaire's footfalls behind him as she approached.

"Most well-behaved mare a body could ask

for." Gideon turned, smiling and offering his hand. "You must be Blaire Afton."

"I am," she answered, shaking his hand. "And you're Gideon Ironheart, right?"

"So I've heard."

Gus was glad to hear her laugh. "Your reputation precedes you," she said. "I heard someone call you a horse whisperer. So, you whisper to them?"

Gideon shook his head. "Most of so-called whispering is knowing horses. They communicate quite well if you pay attention and, if you listen, they decide to please you. Sort of like cats."

Another laugh emerged from Blaire. Gus felt like a grinning fool, just to hear her so happy.

"Let me introduce you," Gideon said. "Then I'm going to ride her up the road a ways to work out the kinks from being in the trailer. After that, she's yours as long as you need her."

"Somebody say that to me." Dave pretended to groan. "We need horses up here so badly I even took a wild hair and repaired the corral for them. Sell that to the state."

"I would if I could," Gideon answered. "I've got some fine mounts that would love working up here."

Gus and Dave helped him open the trailer and lower the ramp, then Gideon stepped inside and led an absolutely gorgeous chestnut out of the trailer.

"Oh, wow," Blaire breathed.

Gideon walked her slowly in a circle, leading her by a rein, then brought her toward Blaire. "Get to know her. Pat her neck first, don't approach her from the front until she gets to know you. Remember, she's got a big blind spot in front of her nose. And talk to her so she'll recognize your voice."

Blaire apparently didn't feel any reluctance to make friends with the horse. She wasn't quite as big as Scrappy, but still large. But then, Blaire had ridden in Afghanistan so this wasn't exactly utterly new to her.

It wasn't long before it became evident that Lita liked Blaire. Five minutes later, the horse wound her neck around and over Blaire's neck and shoulder, a horse hug.

"There you go," said Gideon. "She's yours now. Need anything in the way of supplies?"

Gus recited the list of items he'd brought with him, from bags of feed to grooming supplies.

"You'll do," Gideon agreed. "Call me if you need anything at all."

"You could send another horse," Dave laughed. "As long as you're lending them."

NOT TEN MINUTES after Gideon drove off, Dave helped carry the groceries inside, then left to spend the evening at home. He once again promised to take over for Blaire the next day if needed.

Blaire swiftly put away the groceries with an obliging Gus's help. Then the Conard County deputy arrived.

A big man, appearing to be in his sixties, he unfolded from the SUV. He had long inky hair streaked with gray, and his Native American ancestry was obvious in his face. He looked at them from dark eyes and smiled.

"Micah Parish," he said, shaking their hands. "I saw my brother headed on out." He pointed with his chin toward Lita. "New acquisition?"

"A loaner," Blaire answered. "You're storied in these parts, and I don't even spend that much time in town so I don't get all the gossip."

Micah chuckled, a deep rumbling sound. "I'm storied because I broke some barriers around here."

Gus doubted that was the only reason.

"You talked to my daughter-in-law, Connie," he said. "And, of course, she talked to me. Then Gage talked to me. Seems like folks are worried this murder might be linked to others in the mountains. So, I'm here to share information. Thing is, Gus, I was sent first to you. Somebody's nervous about the national forest."

"The killer, you mean?" Gus frowned. "Has there been a threat?"

"No." Micah looked at Blaire. "You got maps of the whole area?"

"How much do you want?"

"Most of the mountain range on up to Yellowstone."

"On my wall. Come in. Do you want some coffee?"

"My wife, Faith, tells me the day I turn down coffee I'll be at the Pearly Gates."

She pointed him to the large map hanging on the wall and went to start a pot of coffee. For a minute or so, there was silence from the front room, then Micah and Gus began to talk.

"The thing here is this," Micah said. "Can't imagine why no one noticed it before. Hey, Blaire?"

"Yes?" She punched the button to start the pot, then came round into the front room.

"Okay to use the pushpins to mark the map?"

"Go ahead." She didn't usually do that, but the map wasn't inviolate. There was a corkboard beside it, and other than an announcement of a campfire group every Friday evening, it was simply covered with colored pushpins.

Micah pulled a pad out of his jacket pocket and flipped it open. Then he read from it and began sticking red pushpins into the map along the mountain range. "Nobody's perfect," he remarked as he stuck the last pin in place. "I can only approximate the GPS readings on this map."

He stepped back a bit. "These are in order,

marking those five murders that everyone is worried about." He pointed to the highest pin. "Number one."

Then as his finger trailed down along the pins to the one in the state campground, he called the order. There was no mistaking it. The murders had moved southward through the mountains.

"As you can see, it's not anywhere near a perfect line, but it's too close to ignore. All of the victims were isolated, but *not* alone. Like the one in your campground, Blaire. It's as if the killer wanted the body to be found immediately."

She nodded, feeling her skin crawl.

"Anyway," Micah continued, "Gage sent me to warn you, Gus, because the forest might be next in line. Although what you can do about it, I don't know. That's a whole lot of territory. But judging by the previous timing, the threat won't be too soon. You'll have time to figure out what you can do."

"What I can do?" Gus repeated. "Right now I must have thirty hikers out in the woods, plus about sixty families camping mostly at the southern side. I can't just empty the park indefinitely. Not even for this. Damn, I can hear HQ hit the roof."

Micah smiled faintly. "So can I. All you can do is have your people remain alert. These instances might not even be linked. There sure hasn't been anything like the Jasper murder with a kid in the tent."

Blaire had been studying the map closely and eventually spoke. "It looks as if someone is trying to make these events appear random."

The men looked again, and both nodded.

"Not doing very well," Gus remarked.

"Actually, take a closer look. Every one of these killings occurred in a different jurisdiction, including two that happened across the state line. That would make linking them very difficult because the different jurisdictions operate independently. That's clever."

"If it's one killer," agreed Micah.

"It looks," said Gus, "like a carefully planned operation."

Silence fell among the three of them. Blaire's skin tightened the way it often had before going on a transport mission, knowing that danger lay ahead, but having no idea what kind, or from where.

Micah muttered, "Well, hell," as he stared at the map. "That would explain a lot." He faced them. "Gage was going to send you some of the reports, the ones he can get. I'm not sure who'll bring them up or when. Most of these cases are cold and getting colder. And from what he said, none of them have any evidence except bodies. Very useful."

"But there are two murders every summer, right?" Blaire asked. "That's what I heard."

"So it appears, not that you can be sure of much with a sample set of five. All right, I'll head back on down and pass this information to Gage. Good thinking, Blaire. You may have hit on something important."

"Important but probably useless," she responded. "Somebody with brains is behind this but finding that brain isn't going to get any easier."

"Maybe that'll change," Gus offered. "We might find something useful in our survey over the next few days. Or just thinking about all the murders from the perspective you provided might generate some ideas."

"Criminal masterminds," Micah rumbled, and half snorted. "Word is they don't exist."

Blaire couldn't suppress a smile. "That's what they say. They also say that every perp brings something to the scene and leaves something behind. Nobody's apparently found anything left behind except bodies and the bullets in them. Oh, and one shell casing."

"Yeah. The reports will verify it when Gage gets them, but from what he mentioned this morning to me, all the weapons were different, too. God help us."

Micah stayed just long enough to finish a mug of coffee, then headed back down the mountain toward town. Gus helped Blaire with grooming

Lita and feeding her, along with taking care of Scrappy, and she had to admit a certain excitement at the prospect of riding around the mountains with him in the morning.

It had been a long time since she'd been in the saddle, and she'd realized during those days in Afghanistan that she really loved to ride, that she enjoyed the companionship of a horse, and that a horse could be as much of an early warning system as a trained dog. They reacted to strangers by getting nervous, for one thing.

When the horses were taken care of, they headed back inside. "I need a shower," Blaire remarked. "I smell like horse. And since you were here last night, you probably are starting to feel truly grungy."

"I'm used to grungy," he reminded her. "But I'll never turn down a hot shower. You go first."

"It's a luxury, isn't it?"

She'd never realized just how much of one it was until those long missions in the 'Stan. Sometimes she'd felt as if dust and dirt had filled her pores and could never be scrubbed out. She ran upstairs to get clean clothes.

She would have liked to luxuriate in the shower, but she needed to save hot water for Gus. Making it quick, she toweled off swiftly and climbed into fresh jeans and a long-sleeved polo with the state park logo on the shoulder. From the tiny linen cupboard, she pulled out fresh towels for him and placed them on a low stool she kept in the corner for holding her clothes.

In the front room, she found Gus unpacking fresh clothes from a saddlebag.

"Always ready?" she asked lightly.

"That's the Coast Guard, but yeah. A change of clothes is always a handy thing to have around. I'll hurry."

"I'm done. If you want to use up all the hot water, be my guest."

He laughed, disappearing down the short, narrow hallway from the kitchen into her bathroom. A short while later she heard the shower running.

Now to think of dinner. Fortunately that had been at the back of her mind while she'd been shopping, and it was easy enough to choose a frozen lasagna and preheat the oven. She'd gotten lazy. She could have cooked for two, but in the summers she avoided cooking even for herself, except when her freezer gave her fits. She had plastic containers full of things like pea soup and stew on her refrigerator shelf, but none of them held enough for two. The lasagna did.

Gus apparently believed in conserving water, because he emerged from the bathroom, his hair still wet and scented like her bar soap, before the oven beeped that it was preheated.

He looked over her shoulder, giving her the full force of his delightful aromas. "Oh, yum," he said. "I assume you're making dinner?"

"I wouldn't make this much just for me."

He laughed. "So you were thinking about me when we were at the store."

She was thinking about him a lot, she admitted to herself. Maybe too much. But she could deal with that later once things settled down around here.

She put the lasagna in the oven, still covered by its plastic sheeting per directions, then filled their mugs with more coffee. "Front room?" she asked.

"Let me go hang up this towel." He pulled it from around his neck. "Be right there."

She carried the coffee out to the front room, placing his cup on the rustic end table and hers on the counter that separated the room from the workspace. Everything here was rustic, which she liked, but it also felt empty without the usual comings and goings of campers.

She settled behind the counter on her swiveling stool, feeling it might be a safer move than sitting beside him on the sofa. She didn't know why she needed to feel safe as he posed no threat to anything except possibly her peace of mind.

Afraid of damaging their friendship, she didn't want him to even guess how sexually attractive she found him. The pull hadn't worn off with familiarity, either. It seemed to be growing, and in the last couple of days it had grown by leaps and bounds.

He joined her just a few minutes later and dropped onto the couch. "Okay," he said. "There's one thing I want to know, and I want complete truth."

Her heart skipped a beat and discomfort made her stomach flutter. "That sounds ominous."

"It's not." He waved a hand before picking up his coffee mug and toasting her with it in a silent *thank-you.* "I just want to know if I'm driving you nuts by hovering. You're a very capable woman. You don't need a man for much."

She nearly gaped at him, then laughed. "Sexist much?"

"I don't want you to think I'm *being* sexist," he answered. "That's all."

"Ah." She bit her lower lip, but she felt like smiling. "I don't. I just thought you were being a concerned friend."

"Okay, then. It's just that you've taken care of yourself in some pretty sketchy places and situations. I *know* that, and I don't underrate it."

She nodded, liking him even more, if that was possible. "Thank you, but I'm glad you've decided to help. How much ground can I cover alone? And to be quite honest, I feel uneasy. *Really* uneasy. This whole situation stinks, and I don't care how many pins have marked that map, how do we know the killer has moved on? He might hang out in the woods. And if I were to go start poking around by myself, I might make him nervous enough to act, but he might hesitate if I'm not alone. Heck, despite what Micah Parish pointed out with those pins, how can I know I don't make an attractive target out here if I'm by myself?"

"That's my fear," he admitted. "My main fear. This guy obviously likes killing. You might look like a pear ready to pluck."

"I hear most serial killers escalate, too. Speed up." She leaned forward, her elbows on the polished pine counter, and wrapped her hands around her mug. "I've always hated being blind and I was on too many missions where we were just that—blind and waiting for something to happen. That's what this feels like."

"I hear you." Leaning back on the sofa, he crossed his legs, one ankle on the other knee. "I don't like this whole thing. One bit. I could be completely off track, though. Comparing this to anything we went through overseas on missions might really be stretching it. Those instincts could be completely wrong."

"But what are they telling you?"

"Probably the same thing yours are. There's something more than a single murder going on, and I don't mean five of them." He drummed his fingers on his thigh. "That was a really interesting point you made about the murders all being in different jurisdictions. It's not like there's a free flow of crime information between them.

Not unless someone has reason to believe the crimes are linked, or they know the perp has crossed jurisdictional lines."

She nodded. "That was my understanding."

"Cops are like anyone else, they're protective of their turf."

"They don't even like the FBI, from what I hear."

"And if this really does cross state lines, the Bureau could get involved. Another reason not to open their eyes."

"Gage has."

"Gage was a Fed once himself," Gus replied. "I suspect he's less turf conscious than many."

Shaking her head, she tried to ease the tension that was growing in her neck. "There are moments when I feel as if I'm overreacting. I have no more evidence that this killer might act around here again than we have evidence period. And it's driving me nuts not to know a damn thing about why or how this happened."

He put his coffee aside and rose. "Neck tight?"

"Like a spring."

He came around behind her and began to massage her shoulders and neck. "Tell me if I press too hard or it hurts."

At that all she could do was groan with the pleasure of it. "Don't stop."

"I won't. You're tight as a drum."

She could well believe it. Part of her couldn't

let this go, couldn't just brush it off. The police were dealing with it. The other part of her wouldn't just leave it alone. They needed more than a spent shell casing. A whole lot more, and if some guy had watched the campsite long enough to know how to approach and when, then he must have left something behind. *Something*. She knew optics, knew how far it was possible to see with a good scope or binoculars. He could have been more than a hundred yards away. All he needed was a sight line.

Her neck was finally letting go. Her head dropped forward and she felt the release. "Thank you."

"Okay now?"

"Yup. For now."

Dinner was ready. The oven timer beeped, letting her know. "Hungry?" she asked.

"Famished. And I suggest an early night. We should start at first light."

FROM THE WOODS farther up the road, in the trees, Jeff watched in frustration. Wasn't that ranger ever going to go back to his own park? He was all over Blaire like white on rice.

He'd been told he needed to take Blaire out, but he wasn't at all sure she'd even remember their brief encounter or connect him to any of this. Why should she?

But he knew why he was here. This was his

punishment for having lost that shell casing. This was his punishment because he'd known Blaire long ago. He shouldn't have told the guys that he'd passed her on his first recon out here. Hell, she hadn't recognized him then. He was probably just another face among hundreds she saw every summer, and he hadn't really noticed her. Why would she remember him any better than he'd remembered her?

But he had his marching orders. Kill or be killed. Damn, damn, damn, how had he walked into this mess? How had he honestly believed his friends were just playing a game? He should have known Will better. Should have recognized the cold streak in him.

Should have? Psychopaths were notorious for being able to hide their missing empathy, for seeming like people you really wanted to know. So many were successful con men because they appeared so warm and likable. Hard for a mere friend to begin to suspect such a thing.

But that was Jeff's conclusion now, too late. And Karl was probably no better, or else how could they have turned this "game" so deadly? He'd been wrestling with that since he had first realized what was going on, but almost immediately they'd snared him right into this mess. His life or someone else's.

He wished he had more guts. Evidently, for him anyway, it took less guts to shoot someone else.

So now here he was, under orders to kill Blaire Afton, which he *really* didn't want to do, and she might as well have a bodyguard. What was he supposed to do? Take them both out?

He ground his teeth together and leaned his head back against a tree trunk, wishing himself anywhere else on the planet. He couldn't shoot both of them. There was enough of an uproar over the first murder.

And he still had the cries of that child hammering inside his head. He didn't lack feeling the way the other two guys did. He wished he could have shot anyone except a guy with a little kid. Why those two had picked that man...

He'd assumed it was because he was camping alone. And at first he had been, or so it had seemed. Somewhere between the time the details had become fixed and when he'd crept into that campground to shoot the man, a child had arrived. How could he have missed that?

But he knew. In his reluctance to carry out the killing, he hadn't been as attentive as he should have been. No, he'd sat up there higher in the forest, just like this, with his eyes closed, wishing he was in Tahiti, or even the depths of Antarctica.

Reluctantly, he looked again and saw the national forest truck was still parked alongside the state truck. He wondered about the chestnut horse that had been delivered that day and was now out in the corral with the forest ranger's horse.

Maybe the two were lovebirds. Maybe they planned a nice ride in the forest and up the mountainside. Why else would there be another horse in the corral? And if that was the case, how would he ever get Blaire alone so he could shoot her? He sure as hell didn't want another body to add to his conscience.

He ached somewhere deep inside over all this and was beginning to feel that he'd be hurting over this murder until the day he died. Crap, the Jasper guy had been bad. His kid had made it worse. And now he was supposed to kill someone he had actually known however long ago and however briefly?

This time he carried a rifle so he could shoot from a distance, but he also had his pistol. He pulled it out of his holster and stared at it. All he had to do was take himself out and all of this would be over.

He turned it slowly in his hand and thought about how easy it would be. The victim had died instantly. He never moved a muscle, and while Jeff wasn't terribly educated in such things, he had expected at least some twitching or even moaning, shot to the head notwithstanding.

But the kill had apparently been instantaneous. No muscle twitching, no moan, then the kid had started screaming and Jeff had hurried away as fast as he could without pounding the ground with his feet.

As his more experienced "friends" had told him, no one would dare come out to check what had happened for a minute or two, giving him time to slip away. They'd been right. Except for the kid's squalling, the campground had remained silent and still. Confusion and self-protection had reared long enough for Jeff to vanish into the shadows of the night. All without so much as scuffing his feet on the pine needles, dirt and leaves.

No trail. No sound, certainly not with the boy screaming. No evidence other than losing a shell casing.

And now all because of that casing, and the possibility that Blaire might remember his face or name after all these years, he was back here facing another nightmare.

The night was deepening. Lights came on in her cabin. Smoke began to rise from a chimney. It was getting cold out here, so maybe it was cooling down inside.

Maybe, he thought, he ought to try popping her through the window. Sure, and that ranger would come barreling after him instantly.

Nope.

A sound of disgust escaped him, and he brought his weary body to its feet. He had to find a protected spot for the night. He hadn't bothered to locate one while there was still day-light, and through his distress he felt some an-noyance with himself.

He grabbed his backpack with one hand and turned to head deeper into the woods, away from any chance encounter with someone coming up that road. He'd spend another day watching. What choice did he have?

Well, said a little voice in his head, he *could* go back to Will and Karl and confess that he was a complete failure and leave it to them to shoot him.

Except he had a very bad feeling about that. Their little game of not getting caught meant that however they chose to remove him they'd have to make it look like an accident. Which meant he could die in all sorts of ways, from a fire, to a car accident, to a rockfall. Ways that might make him suffer for quite a while.

He wouldn't go out as easily as his own victim had. No way. They'd come up with something diabolical that would keep them in the clear.

It finally was dawning on him that he had plenty of good reason to hate the two men he had always thought were his closest friends. Plenty of reason.

Clouds raced over the moon, occasionally dimming the already darkened woods even more. Each time he had to pause and wait for the light to return. All so he could find a sheltered place where the wind wouldn't beat on him all night and he could bundle up in a sleeping bag.

Maybe his mind would work better in the morning. Maybe he'd find a solution one way or another. A good solution. Hell, maybe he'd find a way out of this altogether.

Vain hope, he supposed. It was hard to hide completely anymore. Very hard. And he had no idea how to stay off the grid.

Damn it all to hell! There had to be a way. And if that way was killing Blaire Afton, what was she to him? Nothing. Not as important as his own life.

Because that's what it really came down to. Who mattered more.

He was almost positive that despite what he'd done, he mattered more. Blaire had gone to war. She probably had a body count that far exceeded anything he could do.

Hell, maybe she even *deserved* to die.

He turned that one around in his head as he finally spread out his sleeping bag against the windbreak of a couple of large boulders.

Yeah. She deserved it.

Now he just had to figure out the best way to do it.

Feeling far better than he had in a couple of days, he curled up in his sleeping bag with some moss for a pillow, and finally, for the first time since he'd killed that guy, he slept well.

Chapter Nine

Dawn was just barely breaking, the first rosy light appearing to the east, as Blaire and Gus made a breakfast of eggs, bacon and toast. They ate quickly, cleaned up quickly, then with a couple of insulated bottles full of coffee, they went out back to the corral and found two horses that looked ready for some action.

Gus helped Blaire saddle Lita, carefully instructing her on the important points of the western saddle. They weren't so very different from the saddle she had used a few times in Afghanistan.

He saddled Scrappy with practiced ease, and soon they were trotting up the road toward the rustic campsite where a man had been killed. They hadn't talked much, but Gus wasn't naturally chatty in the morning, and Blaire didn't seem to be, either.

The horses seemed to be enjoying the climb,

prancing a bit, tossing their heads and whinnying once in a while as if talking to one another.

"I hope you slept well," Blaire said, breaking the prolonged silence. "That couch is barely long enough for you. Oh, heck, it's not long enough at all."

"It was fine. And yeah, I slept well. You?"

"Nightmares." She shook her head as if she could shake loose of them.

"About anything in particular?"

"I wish I knew. No, just woke up with the sensation of having spent a frightening night. I probably ought to be glad I can't remember. For too long, I could."

He knew exactly what she meant. Long after coming home, long after returning to civilian life, he'd relived some of his worst experiences in his dreams. "This situation hasn't been good for the mental health."

"No," she admitted. "I'm beginning to feel as if I'm teetering on a seesaw between the past and present." She paused. "Hey, that's exactly the thing I've been describing as being uneasy. I just realized it. Yeah, there was a murder, it was heinous, but that alone can't explain why tension is gripping me nearly every single minute."

"Maybe it could." But he didn't believe it.

Another silence fell, and he would have bet that she was considering her post-traumatic stress and how this event might have heightened it.

Everyone had it to some degree. Some were luckier, having it in smaller bits they could more easily ignore. Some couldn't get past it at all. He figured he was somewhere in the middle, and after all this time he had a better handle on it. Hell, he and Blaire had spent hours over coffee discussing it, as if talking about it would make those memories and feelings less powerful.

Maybe it had. The last few months he'd thought the two of them were moving to a better place. Now this. Not a better place at all.

When they reached the turn to the rustic campground, they paused. "Want to look over the scene again?" he asked her.

"I'm thinking. How much could the crime scene techs have missed? They certainly found the shell casing."

"True. So let's start circling farther out."

But she chose to circle the evident edge of the camping area, with all the sites in clear view. She drew rein at one point and looked down.

Gus followed her gaze and saw the small metal cars in the dirt, roadways still evident. Kids playing. Kids whose parents had been stricken enough by events that they'd left without getting these toys. Maybe the youngsters had been upset enough not to care about them, or had even forgotten them in the ugliness of what had occurred.

"Sad," Blaire remarked.

"Yeah."

They continued on their way, and through the trees he could see the tent where the man had been killed, and the crime scene tape that still surrounded the area. He wondered if anyone would clean that up or if it would be left to Blaire and her staff.

He asked, "Are they done with the scene?"

"I don't know. I need to ask. Then I guess we get to do the cleanup."

That answered his question. "I'll help."

She tossed him a quizzical look. "I thought you had your own responsibilities."

"I do, but Holly's in her element. She always enjoys standing in for me. One of these days, I bet she replaces me."

That drew a smile from Blaire and he was relieved to see it. She'd been awfully somber this morning.

After the first circuit, during which they'd noted nothing of interest, they moved out another fifty yards. The woods grew thicker but when he looked uphill, he saw more than one potential sight line. Not far enough, maybe, before they were blocked by the growth, but they were still there. He felt, however, that a watcher would have stationed himself a much longer way out if he could. Away from chance discovery.

"Kids like to run in the woods," Blaire remarked. "Several times a year we have to go looking for them. You?"

"No different for us."

"They're usually farther out than this. Far enough that they completely lose sight of the camp. Too much of a chance that someone would stumble over our killer here."

"The same thought crossed my mind."

Another smile from her. "Well, we're on the same wavelength quite a bit."

"So it seems." Mental echoes of one another at times. When he wasn't appreciating it, he could become amused by it. Right now he knew exactly what she was doing when she moved her reins to the left and headed them uphill.

"Hundred yards next?" he asked.

"Yes, if you agree."

"Why wouldn't I?" He was enjoying her taking charge and doing this her way. He'd never minded women being in charge, even though he hadn't come across it often in spec ops, and he had no trouble seeing Blaire as a complete equal. They'd walked the same roads, to some extent, and shared a lot of experience. Now they even had similar civilian jobs.

The only thing that troubled him was the attraction that kept goading him. Boy, that could blow things up fast. Then there was the protectiveness he was feeling. Even though she had said she didn't mind him hanging around, he had to hope she wasn't beginning to feel like he didn't trust her to take care of herself.

That would be demeaning. Not at all what he wanted her to feel.

They reached a point on the second circle where she drew rein sharply. He paused, just behind her, and strained his senses when she said nothing. Waiting, wondering if she had heard or seen something.

Then he noticed it, too. At first the jingle and creak of harness and saddle had made him inattentive to sound, but now that it was gone, he could hear it. Or not hear it as the case was.

She turned Lita carefully until she could look at him sideways. "The birds."

He nodded. They had fallen silent.

"Could be a hiker," she said quietly. "I don't have any registered at the moment, but simple things like letting someone know where you're going up here don't always seem important to people."

"I know," he answered just as quietly. "Not until we have to send out huge search parties to hunt for someone with a sprained ankle who can barely tell us which quadrant he's in. Don't you just love it?" Then he fell silent, too, listening.

A breeze ruffled the treetops, but that was nothing new. The air was seldom still at that height, although here at ground level it could often become nearly motionless because of the tree trunks and brush.

None of that explained the silence of the birds, however. No, that indicated major disturbance, and he doubted he and Blaire were causing it, or they'd have noticed it earlier.

Problem was, he couldn't imagine what could be causing the unusual silence. The birds were used to ordinary animals and threats in the woods, and if the two of them on horseback hadn't silenced them, what had?

Another glance at Blaire told him the silence was concerning her. The birds had to feel threatened.

Then, almost in answer to the thought, a boom of thunder rolled down the mountainside.

"Great time for Thunder Mountain to live up to its reputation," Blaire said.

They both looked up and realized the sky just to the west had grown threateningly inky. It was going to be bad.

"Better head back," he said.

She nodded reluctantly.

He understood. This search of theirs had only just begun, and now they were having to cut it short. Who could guess how much evidence might be wiped away by a downpour. Probably anything that there might be.

She started to turn Lita, then paused.

He eased Scrappy up beside her, trying to

ignore the electric tingle as their legs brushed briefly. "What?" he asked.

"I just felt…something. The back of my neck prickled. Probably the coming storm." She shrugged and started her mount back toward the road.

Gus followed. Her neck had prickled? He knew that feeling and he seriously doubted it was the storm.

Growing even more alert, he scanned the woods around them. He didn't see a damn thing.

HELL'S BELLS, JEFF THOUGHT. He saw the growing storm, although he doubted it would hit that quickly. What annoyed the dickens out of him was that the two were headed away, probably back to the cabin. He couldn't keep up with those horses unless he tried to run, and he figured he'd either make too much noise and be heard, or he'd break an ankle and die out here.

Regardless, any chance he might have found to take out Blaire was lost for now. Instead he had to figure out how to weather this storm without freezing to death. Nobody needed to draw him a map about how dangerous it was to get wet up here. He'd done enough hunting to know.

Having to hunker under a survival blanket while trying to keep his gear dry and hoping he hadn't chosen a place where he'd quickly be sitting in runoff didn't please him one bit.

Thunder boomed again, hollow but louder. Time to take cover, and quickly. He found himself a huge boulder that looked as if it sank into the ground enough to prevent a river from running under it and began to set up his basic camp. Only as he was spreading his survival blanket, however, did he realize it had a metallic coating.

Damn! Would it be enough to attract lightning? Or would he be safe because of the high trees and the boulder? Except he knew you shouldn't shelter under trees during a storm. So where the hell was he supposed to go?

The first big raindrop that hit his head told him he was out of time. He'd just have to set up here, and if he was worried about the survival blanket maybe he shouldn't use it. Just sit here and get drenched and hope the rain didn't penetrate his backpack. Out of it, he pulled a waterproof jacket that was too warm for the day, but it might be all he had to prevent hypothermia in a downpour.

Or use the damn blanket, he argued with himself. Getting struck by lightning would at least get him out of this mess. It would probably be a much better end than going back to his so-called friends without having completed this task.

Task. Murder. *Might as well face it head-on, Jeff,* he said to himself, then spoke aloud. "You're a killer now. You killed a man you didn't even know for no good reason at all except to save your own damn neck."

The woods had lost their ability to echo anything back at him. Maybe it was the growing thickness of the air, or the rain that had begun to fall more steadily. The only good thing he could say about it was that any evidence he'd left behind would be washed away.

He pulled the survival blanket out of his backpack and unfolded it, tucking it around himself and his gun and gear. A bolt of lightning would be a good thing right now.

And he didn't give a damn that this blanket must stick out like a sore thumb. Somebody finding him and taking him in for any reason at all would be almost as good as a lightning strike.

Miserable, hating himself, hating the weather, he hunkered inside the blanket.

BLAIRE HELPED GUS as much as she could with the horses. The saddles went under the lean-to to be covered with a tarp that was folded in there. The horses… Well, horses had withstood far worse for millennia, but Gus left the wool saddle blanket on their backs and gently guided them under the lean-to.

Blaire patted Lita on the neck and murmured to her. Her flanks quivered a bit as the thunder boomed, but she remained still.

"If they were free, they'd run," Gus said. "Unfortunately, I can't let them do that. They could get hurt on this ground."

She nodded, stroking Lita's side. "They'll be okay?"

"Sure. I'm positive Lita has been through storms at Gideon's ranch, and I know for a fact Scrappy's been through a bunch of them. I just want them to feel comfortable under the lean-to."

She nodded. "And if they get wet…"

"The wool saddle blankets will help keep them warm. They'll be fine, Blaire. Scrappy's never been pampered and I'm sure Gideon doesn't have enough barn space to bring his animals inside. Nope, they'll withstand it. Unlike us. Can we make some coffee?"

She laughed and led the way inside, but she honestly wasn't feeling very good. This storm threatened to kill any possibility of finding some evidence to help locate the killer. Maybe they'd been asking for too much. "Gus? Espresso or regular?"

"I could use espresso for the caffeine, but on the other hand regular might give me an excuse to drink more hot liquid, and I feel like I'm getting a little chilled."

"You, too? I think the temperature must have dropped twenty degrees while we were riding back. Maybe we'll need a fire." Then she put her hands on her hips and tipped her head quizzically. "So, coffee? Espresso or regular?"

He grinned. "That was an evasion. I can't make up my mind. Whichever you want."

"Some help."

He followed her around to the kitchen. "Want me to bring in some wood? And do you want the fire in the fireplace or in the woodstove?"

The cabin had both. Blaire didn't know the history, but there was a nice stone fireplace next to a Franklin stove that could really put out the heat. She preferred the stove in the winter, but right now it wasn't that cold.

"Let's start with the fireplace, if that's okay."

"More romantic."

She froze as that comment dropped, but he was already on his way out to get wood. What had he meant by that? Anything? Nothing?

Dang. Her heart started beating a little faster as she wondered if he'd been joking. Since first meeting him, she'd been quashing the attraction she felt toward him, but it was very much alive and well. Those simple words had nearly set off a firestorm in her.

More romantic?

Oh, she wished.

With effort, she focused her attention on making a pot of fresh regular coffee. If he still wanted more caffeine later, it wasn't hard to make espresso.

GUS GAVE HIMSELF quite a few mental kicks in the butt as he gathered logs and kindling into a large tote clearly made for the task. Hadn't he seen a wood box inside? In a corner on the front side of the room? Serving as an extra seat beneath a tattered cushion? Maybe he should have checked that out first.

But after what had slipped out of his mouth, he was glad to be out here under the small lean-to alongside the cabin. The corral was out back with another lean-to, but this was the woodshed, capable of holding enough fuel for an entire winter. Right now he looked at nearly six cords of dry wood. Good enough.

He took more time than necessary because if he'd walked out on a mess of his own making with his casual comment, he needed a way to deal with it. Problem was, that would all depend on how she had reacted to it. Maybe she'd taken it as a joke. He half hoped so, even though truth had escaped his lips.

A fire in the fireplace *would* be more romantic. The question was whether this was the time or place. Or even the right relationship. She might be no more eager than he to risk their friendship.

And romance could tear it asunder if it didn't work out. Funny thing about that, how a relationship that could be so close could also be a godawful mess if it went awry.

He ought to know. He hadn't spent his entire life living like a monk. He'd had girlfriends. He'd considered asking one of them to marry him, too. He thought he'd found true love at last. Just like a soap opera.

And just like a soap opera it had turned out that when he was away on assignment, she liked to fool around. Being alone wasn't her cup of tea at all.

That one had hurt like hell. Mostly the betrayal, he'd decided later. He couldn't even be sure afterward that he'd really loved her. Maybe he'd been more in love with the idea of having a wife, and maybe a kid or two, and coming home after a mission to a family.

It was possible. He might well have deluded himself.

Or possibly he'd been every bit as scorched as he'd felt.

Inside he found Blaire heating up canned clam chowder as if nothing had happened.

"If you're allergic to shellfish, tell me now," she said. "I can make you something else."

"Not allergic, thank God. Life without shellfish would suck."

She laughed lightly as he went out to the fireplace and built a nice fire on the hearth. When he finished, he had a nice blaze going and she'd placed bowls of soup, a plate of crackers and some beer on the kitchenette table, where he was able to join her.

"If the bowls weren't so hot, I'd suggest eating in front of the fire," she said. "You did a nice job."

"You do a nice job of heating up canned soup," he retorted, drawing another laugh out of her. Man, he loved that sound.

"Yeah. I'm not much of a cook. Mom tried to teach me, but I felt no urge to put on an apron."

Which might be what led her to the military. No standard role for this woman. He liked it.

After dinner he insisted on taking care of washing up. When he'd dried his hands and came out to the front room, he found her staring at the map Micah Parish had stuck with pins.

"It's a definite plan," she murmured.

"I agree," he said, coming up beside her.

"But the killings are so far apart in time as well as location, there's no reason to expect him to act again anytime soon."

"You wouldn't think."

"So he's atypical for a serial murderer. Not escalating."

"Not yet anyway."

She turned her head to look at him. "This is so stupid, feeling uneasy that he might be hanging around. He's probably gone home to think about his next move."

"Maybe."

She arched a brow. "Maybe?"

He shook his head a little. "This guy appears to be smart, unless this is all chance," he said, pointing at the map.

"But if he *is* smart?"

"Then what better way to throw us off than by breaking the pattern?"

She caught her breath. "So I'm not crazy."

"Did I say you were?"

She shook her head and faced him. "You feel it, too."

"Call it combat sense. I don't know. I've got this itch at the base of my skull that won't leave me alone. I tried to act like the murder was over, the guy had gone away. That's why it took me two days to start hovering around you. Because I can't escape the feeling that this isn't over. Don't ask me why. It's just there, an itch. A sting like a pinprick in my brain. Anyway, there's no one else here for him to go after, so I started worrying about you."

She dropped her head, looking down at the wooden floor. "Yeah. From the outset I haven't been able to shake it. Something about that murder... My God, Gus, I can't get over it. What kind of monster shoots a sleeping man when his small son is right beside him? He's got no limit, evidently. So what next? My seasonal staff?"

"Or you," he said quietly.

She whipped around and faced the fire, placing her hands on her hips. It was a defiant pose, he thought.

"Let him try," she said. "Besides, this is all speculation."

But neither of them believed it. Not completely. Finely honed senses were pinging and couldn't be ignored.

WILL WAS FED UP with Jeff. He didn't bother to discuss it with Karl. He didn't want any kind of debate, even though he and Karl were very much on the same wavelength.

Jeff must be dealt with. Not necessarily killed but hamstrung enough that he'd never murmur a word about any of this. And while Karl might think that being responsible for one murder would be enough to shut him up, Will didn't.

Damn, he hated overdeveloped consciences.

He, Jeff and Karl had been friends since early childhood. Their fathers had been hunting buddies and when the boys were old enough, they'd joined the hunts with them. Always spending a few weeks here at this lodge, sharing plenty of laughter, talk and beer. It had never occurred to him that friendship with Jeff could become an Achilles' heel.

Of course, when he'd started this damn game, he'd never intended to start killing, so it had never struck him it might be best not to mention it to Jeff.

So he'd sat here in this very chair shooting off his mouth about a game. All because he'd recently come across the story of Leopold and Loeb and had wondered if the three of them could prove they were smarter. Actually, it wasn't really a question, because Leopold and Loeb had been nowhere near as smart as they had believed.

Still, it had been intended to be a game, just as he had said that night. For a while, the stalking and planning had been enough, but then one night Karl had said, "The thrill is going away."

Fateful words. The first few times, they'd simply shot to miss, to cause a bad scare. And they'd been careful not to let Jeff know what was up, because they'd learned long ago that Jeff's conscience was probably bigger than Jeff himself. Besides, they knew him for a weakling. He hated confrontation, and when they were kids he'd been inclined to run away rather than stand up for himself.

Wimp.

So now here they were. They'd managed to pressure Jeff into killing one man just to make it impossible for him to run to the cops. But had they *really* made it impossible?

He had sensed Jeff's fear. Not that Jeff's being afraid was anything new, but the guy was afraid that he and Karl would kill *him*. They would if it became necessary. Regardless, he and Karl were certain they'd left no traces behind so even if Jeff went running to the cops, they could claim they knew nothing at all and Jeff must have gone nuts.

After all, they were, every one of them, respectable people without police records. He and Karl were pillars of their community. Jeff was... well, an underachiever. Not a man to like taking risks even to get ahead.

Now this. Jeff had been in the Army with that ranger woman. She'd glimpsed him on their first survey trip when they'd gone to pick the campground for the hit. He said he was sure she hadn't recognized him.

But Jeff had recognized *her* and that stuck in Will's craw like a fish bone. Not good.

Karl didn't like it, either. There was a link now, and Jeff was that link. They either had to get rid of Jeff or get rid of the ranger. Neither of them especially wanted to kill Jeff. He'd been part of their entire lives, and his father had been like a beloved uncle to them.

But one or the other had to go. If that woman ranger remembered Jeff being there, and found just one thing, anything, that made her draw a connection, there was going to be hell to pay.

Jeff had called just an hour ago on the sat phone, telling Will that a thunderstorm had him pinned down and he couldn't act tonight, especially with another ranger there. Will figured he just needed some goading.

For Pete's sake, pinned down by a freaking

thunderstorm? Jeff needed to grow some cojones. If there were two rangers there, so what? Take them both out, then get the hell out of there. At the least, it would make this case stand out from the others in case the growing talk made the authorities think about the murders being linked.

Frustration with Jeff was nothing new these days. Will growled to himself, then pulled his tablet out of its case and looked at the map on which he'd been following Jeff's every move. Jeff had no idea that Will and Karl could track him, not that it probably mattered to him.

But it mattered to Will and Karl. If the man took a hike anywhere near a cop, they wanted to be able to step in. So far Jeff hadn't entertained any such thoughts, at least none that he'd evinced.

But that didn't ease Will's frustration any. He and Karl had agreed that after this murder they needed to take some time off. Maybe a couple of years. Find another way to amuse themselves. If they did that, any links someone might perceive would go up in smoke.

He settled back in his chair, puffing on his cigar, staring at the red blinking dot on his map. It came and went, but he was fairly certain that was because the wimp was huddling under a survival blanket, hiding from the rain. Each time the dot returned, it assured him that Jeff hadn't moved.

But damn it, Jeff, he thought. The rain would make a perfect cover to just get the job done. No one would hear a thing. It was likely any evidence would just wash away if the downpour was as heavy as Jeff had said.

He was also fairly certain that Jeff wouldn't leave another shell casing behind. So, use the high power rifle and take out the rangers and get out of the rain.

Sometimes Jeff didn't think too well.

Hell, maybe most of the time.

Will set the tablet aside and sat smoking his cigar with one hand and drumming his fingers with the other. He needed a way to motivate Jeff. Soon. This couldn't continue as long as there was a whisper of a chance that that ranger might remember him somehow, especially if his name came up. If the cops had found some kind of evidence.

Will sat forward suddenly, unpleasant feelings running down his spine. If Jeff had left behind a shell casing, maybe he'd left even more behind. He clearly hadn't been cautious enough.

Well, of course not. The wimp had been afraid. He'd scurried away leaving that casing behind and who knew what else. One of his cigarette butts? God knew how the police might be able to use something like that.

He picked up the sat phone and called Jeff. "Still raining?" he asked. He hoped so.

God, maybe he should just go out there, kill Jeff himself, then take out the ranger to be extra careful. Yeah, somehow make Jeff nearly impossible to identify because he *could* be linked to Karl and Will.

Hell! He was beginning to think more like a movie or television show. What was he going to do? Murder Jeff, cut off his fingers and face, then murder a ranger so she wouldn't suddenly remember Jeff's name?

No, Jeff was supposed to kill the ranger, tie up the last important loose end, and it was the least he could do considering he'd left that damn shell casing behind. First rule in this game: leave nothing behind. Nothing.

Jeff answered, his voice shaking.

"Why are you shaking?" Will demanded.

"Cold," came the abbreviated answer.

"Man up," Will said shortly. "Take advantage of the rain and just take the woman out. Then you can get inside again and warm your delicate toesies."

"Shut up," Jeff said. It sounded as if he'd gritted the words out between his teeth.

"I will not shut up. I might, however, come out there and kill you myself to close this out."

Complete silence answered him. Then, suddenly, he clearly heard the sound of rain beating on the survival blanket for just a few seconds before the line went empty. He glanced at the tablet and saw that Jeff had disappeared again. The son of a gun had cut him off. Probably deliberately.

But no, a few seconds later he heard Jeff's voice again and saw the dot reappear on the map.

"I'll get her tomorrow," he said. "And you know what, Will?"

God it was almost impossible to understand Jeff with his voice shaking like that. "What?"

"She saw me, all right. I don't think she recognized my face but she might have. Anyway, she knows we went up there five days before I killed that guy, and at some point she's going to put that together."

Will felt stunned. Ice water trickled down his spine. "You lie."

"No, I lied the first time. I don't trust you, and I didn't want to kill *her*, and now that's exactly where I am because you and Karl are goddamn psychopaths who don't give a flying fig about anyone else on this planet. I have half a mind to come to the lodge and kill the two of you for getting me into this."

"You don't have the stones."

"Are you sure of that? But to cover my own butt I have to make sure that woman can't put me together with this mess. That's all on you, jerk. All of it. When this is done, I want nothing to do with the two of you ever again. Buy out my share of the lodge, then stay out of my life."

Yeah, like they'd pay him a dime. But now

was not the time to get into that, or even think about it.

"Has it occurred to you," Jeff asked, his voice quavering, "that she may have recognized me, but she also saw the two of you?"

"All the more reason to erase her," Will said sharply.

"No, you're not getting it, you ass. If I turn up dead, she may remember you two and give your descriptions."

That silenced Will. For once he hadn't thought of something.

"And if you think killing me will save you, think again. I turn up dead, everyone knows we're friends... Nah, you'll be under the microscope."

Dang, thought Will, maybe the guy had some stones after all.

Several seconds passed before he spoke again. "Then you'd better take her out and tie off the loose end. We told you that you could be our next target, and we're not stupid. We can make it look like an accident." Will felt his own bravado covering his sudden uncertainty.

"Yeah. Sure."

"Just do it, Jeff."

"I will, damn it. But just leave me alone. I'm not sitting out here in this miserable rain and cold because I enjoy it."

Then he disconnected, leaving Will to listen to the static of a disturbed signal.

After a minute or two, Will put down the phone and picked up his tablet. Jeff was still there. Will looked across the room to the gun rack, which held seven rifles, some good for hunting, but a couple for much longer-range shooting. Damn near sniper rifles. His dad and Karl's had often liked to practice target shooting over a thousand yards.

Jeff had one of those rifles with him right now. He didn't even have to get close to the woman.

But Will thought about going out there and using one of them on Jeff. He studied the map on his tablet, bringing up the terrain. No roads nearby. He'd have to hike through the night, a dangerous thing to do even without a storm.

Hell! He almost hurled the tablet in frustration. If Jeff didn't take that damn woman out by tomorrow night, he and Karl were going to have to do something about Jeff.

No escaping it. Especially since Jeff had pointed out that she'd seen all three of them. They'd have to get rid of him in a way that wouldn't jog her memory so they could stay clear of her.

Or they'd have to kill them both along with that nosy federal ranger.

Either way, if Jeff failed, they'd have to mop up. They should have gotten rid of him as soon as they learned he'd figured out what they were doing. Honoring an old friendship this way had proved to be the biggest headache they'd had so far.

He was coming to hate Jeff.

THE WIND HAD picked up considerably and was blowing rain so hard against the window glass that it sounded like small pebbles.

"Will the horses be okay?" Blaire asked.

"Yeah," Gus said. "They know how to hunker together and they've got pretty thick hides. If they didn't there wouldn't be any horses."

"I guess you're right. I know I wouldn't want to be out there in this."

"Not if I can avoid it," he agreed.

She rubbed her arms as they sat on the couch separated by a couple of feet. "This place doesn't usually feel drafty." She paused. "Let me take that back. It can in the winter because of the temperature differential between the glass and the log walls. That's when I put up the shutters. No shutters tonight."

She had already pulled on a cardigan, but now she rose and went to sit on the rug in front of the fire. Closer to the heat and warmth.

"Is that a wood box over there?" Gus asked.

She twisted and followed his pointing finger. "Yes, it is. I think it's full. I should have mentioned it rather than you going outside to get wood."

"I think by the time I got to the door you were in the kitchen starting soup. It's okay." Rising, he went to the box, lifted the long seat pillow off it and looked inside. "I certainly won't have to go out for more wood tonight."

She pulled her knees up under her chin and wrapped her arms around them. "This fire feels so good. But there went all hope of finding any evidence out there. This rain is heavy enough to wash it all away. And the wind will probably knock down the tent and the crime scene tape. Of course, that'll make the area fresh and clean again."

"There are advantages." He joined her on the floor, sitting cross-legged. "There had to be some place he was hanging out to observe from. I doubt the rain will wash that away. And if we find it, we might find something useful."

She glanced at him. "So you still want to go on the hunt tomorrow?"

"If this weather improves. But absolutely. If you're like me, you want to feel like you're actually accomplishing something, not sitting on your hands. I mean, I'd settle back if the police had the guy."

"So would I. But until then..." She turned her attention back to the fire. "I can't stop hearing that little boy cry. It makes me so mad. Furious. Someone needs to pay."

"Yeah. I'm with you."

Watching the flames leap, she thought about what she'd just revealed to him and herself. It *was* about the boy, she admitted. As much as anything, she wanted that boy to grow up with the satisfaction of knowing his father's killer had been caught and sent to prison. Yeah, she was worried he might still be hanging around, and she couldn't blame Gus for being concerned about her safety. Every night, with the campers all gone, she was out here all alone. It wasn't as if she never needed to emerge from this cabin during the hours when her staff weren't here.

Nope. And if this guy was in it just for the thrill, she'd make a great target. Maybe he even thought she might have found some evidence. After all, she'd been the first person to approach the tent.

"Oh, heck," she said in a burst of frustration. She reclined on the rug, staring up at the dancing shadows on the ceiling. "I hate feeling like everything is messed up and I can't do anything to sort it out. Things were a lot clearer in the Army."

"*Some* things were," he agreed. "But that kind of thinking is what makes it so hard to adjust to the return to civilian life."

"I'm sure. I've been guilty of it more than once." She rolled on her side and propped her chin in her hand. "I don't remember my life before the Army being so messy, but maybe that's not true. No way to tell now. And I'm probably misremembering a lot of things from my military days. Nothing is all that clear-cut."

"Except lines of authority, and even those can get muddy."

He unfolded his legs and stretched out beside her, also propping his chin in his hand. "What I'm trying to think about now is how I'm in a warm cabin with a full belly and a good friend instead of stuck in a frigid cave hoping the paraffin flame will actually make the instant coffee hot."

"Good thoughts," she said after a moment. Then a heavy sigh escaped her. "This is a form of PTSD, isn't it?"

"What is?"

She closed her eyes a moment. "I need to face it. A gun report. A man shot in the head, in vivid Technicolor for me, a crying kid and now I've been paranoid since it happened. The paranoia isn't based in any evidence, merely in my past experience."

She opened her eyes and found him staring at her, appearing concerned, his eyes as gray as the storm outside. He spoke. "Then we're both having PTSD. I feel the paranoia. You might be right. It might be a leftover reaction. But what if it isn't? I'm not prepared to stake everything on dismissing this. It's not like I was walking down a street and heard a backfire. This is a whole different level."

He had a point, but she hated not being able to trust her own judgment. "It's awful," she said frankly. "Not being able to trust myself. It's a new thing."

"You didn't feel this way in Afghanistan?"

"Not often. That's what I meant about everything being so clear. There were bad guys, there were good guys, and if there was any doubt, it didn't last long. But this is different. I'm worrying about the stupidest possible thing. That a killer, who has most likely already moved on so he won't be found, might be stalking *me*. I have absolutely no evidence for that. It's just a feeling. A phantasm."

He reached out to grip her shoulder firmly but gently. "Given how many times a *feeling* has saved my life, I'm not going to dismiss this one, and neither should you. When the guy is locked up, then we can kick our own butts for our reactions. But on the off chance…" He didn't complete the sentence. He just gave her shoulder a squeeze, then let go.

"We're hot messes, Gus," she remarked after a few minutes.

"Sometimes. Not always. We're luckier than a lot of people. Holding steady jobs. Having friends."

"One *real* friend," she said honestly.

He shook his head a little but let it pass. She figured he didn't see any point arguing with the plain truth. She knew a lot of people, but as for counting friends of the kind she could truly share her mind and heart with, Gus was it. He'd been there. He understood. Considering she wasn't a hop away from a support group, Gus was priceless in that regard.

But it was more than his understanding. Gus had been there any time she needed someone. Like now. Running around with this paranoid fear clawing at her, he'd been right beside her, his mere presence making her feel safer.

"Thanks for being you," she said quietly. "Your friendship means the world."

His expression softened from concern. "I could say the same to you. Two slightly bent vets who've spent the last two years sharing things we couldn't share with most people. Then we're pretty much on our own in separate parks, tied up too much to go seeking the company of other vets. There's a support group in town, but how often could we get there? Honestly."

"Not frequently," she admitted. Her days off were generally jam-packed with things she needed to do, and come winter there was often no getting out of here at all. But Gus always managed to find his way over here on Scrappy.

She shifted her position so she could look at the fire again. Staring at him was awakening feelings in her that had absolutely nothing to do with paranoia. She was afraid she might simply leap into his arms.

No time for this, she warned herself. Not now. No way did she want to do something that would make him feel it was necessary to get out of here. He'd never evinced any sexual interest in her that she could be sure of, and she'd been careful to avoid the same.

Sometimes it seemed as if their shared experience was a wall between them. Maybe it was. Who knew what might happen if they knocked down that wall and moved past friendship.

"You ever dated much?" he suddenly asked, surprising her.

She turned to see him. "Yeah. A bit."

"Never found the right one?"

Forgetting her concerns for a moment, she smiled. "Apparently not. You?"

"I got really serious once. It turned out to be a big mistake. When I left town, she found someone else to fill in until I returned."

"Ouch!" She winced. "I don't know that I ever had that going on. Of course, I never got serious. Nobody inspired that in me."

"A tough nut, huh?" But his eyes danced a little.

"Maybe. Or maybe I'm just too damn picky."

"Picky is a good thing to be."

Taking her by surprise, he rolled onto his back,

then drew her toward him until her head rested on his shoulder and his arm wrapped her back.

"Gus?" Her heart leaped with delight.

"A little comfort for us both," he answered. "Not that it's going to last long because the soles of my boots are starting to get too warm. You?"

"Yeah." She gave a quiet little laugh. "At least I'm not cold now."

"Always a good thing. Except those summers when we wished we were on an iceberg."

"Yeah. Huge extremes." Unable to resist, she snuggled a little closer and inhaled his scent. Wonderful. And the way her boots were getting warmer, she figured they'd both be safe. Another couple of minutes and they'd have to back away from the fire or completely change position.

But right now she wanted to revel in the rare experience of physical closeness with another human being. With a man. Since coming home she'd avoided it, feeling that she was too messed up to get involved without hurting someone.

Yeah, she was adapting pretty well, but if her paranoia of the past few days didn't make it clear that she wasn't completely recovered, nothing would.

And if she couldn't trust her own mind and feelings, she wasn't fit to be anyone's companion.

Then she felt her feet. "Aw, damn," she said, pulling away from his delicious embrace and sitting up. If the heat from the fire had penetrated the thick soles of her work boots, it would steadily get hotter for a while, and those soles wouldn't cool down quickly. *Been there, done that,* she thought as she tugged at laces. *Bad timing, though.*

Gus half laughed and sat up, reaching for his own boots. "You're right. I just wasn't ready to let you go."

The words warmed her heart the way the fire had warmed her boots. She tossed him a sideways smile, as she pulled her boots off and set them to one side. Stockinged feet were always comfortable in here unless the floor got really cold. That seldom happened so her feet were generally warm enough.

She realized she was growing thirsty. Beer with dinner had been great, but the soup had been salty as had the crackers. "Something to drink?" she asked.

"Sure." He rose with her and they walked around to the kitchen. "This is sort of like a shotgun house," he remarked.

"I think it was built piecemeal by adding at the back, but I'm not sure. At least I have the loft for a bedroom."

"I bet it's toasty on winter nights."

"Oh, yeah." She opened the refrigerator, revealing a couple of bottles of juice, a few more beers and soft drinks. "Or do you want coffee or tea?"

"I told you I never refuse coffee, but if it's too late for you…"

It wasn't. In fact, it wasn't that late at all, she thought as she glanced at the digital clock on the wall. She turned on the espresso machine, then said, "Latte?"

"Perfect."

Outside, the wind howled and rain beat on the windows, but inside all was warm and dry. Blaire was really glad not to be out there tonight.

Chapter Ten

Jeff had just about had it. After his reaming out over the satellite phone from Will, the person he most wanted to shoot was Will. Followed, probably, by himself.

But neither of those things was going to happen. Nope. Instead he sat there shivering under a survival blanket that, while it was keeping him dry, was too open to keep him warm. The storm had dropped the temperature fast, and at this higher altitude it never got exactly hot to begin with. His fingers, even inside gloves, felt so cold he wondered if he'd get frostbite. Being reduced to eating energy bars didn't help much, either.

But he had to keep the blanket spread to protect his backpack full of essential items, like food and survival equipment, and even though it *shouldn't* make any difference, he didn't want to expose either his rifle or his pistol to the rain. They should still fire, but... What about the scope he might need? It wouldn't help to have it full of water or steamed up when he found his opportunity.

If he ever found his opportunity.

Don't leave a trail or evidence behind. The first rule, one they had repeated until his brain felt like it was being cudgeled. So maybe Blaire had recognized him. It didn't mean she'd connect him to the murder.

But since he'd admitted to knowing her, other thoughts had danced unprompted through his head. Maybe she had recognized him. Maybe she would wonder why he never registered for a campsite or signed in as a hiker. What if, by chance, she put him together mentally with the murder, or simply mentioned it to the law because it started to nag at her.

The way he'd begun to be nagged by the moment of recognition.

Or what if they found a fingerprint on that damn shell casing. She'd recognize his name if they mentioned it to her. Oh, she'd probably be able to tell them more than the Army could after all these years. It hadn't been for long, but they'd trained side by side for a few weeks. How much had he shared with her?

He couldn't recall now. Too long ago, and he hadn't placed any undue emphasis on avoiding chitchat about personal things like families and high schools and other friends. Hell, for all he knew he'd mentioned Will and Karl to her. What if she remembered *that*?

Oh man, maybe he should just risk his neck and slide down this sodden mountain through slippery dirt and duff, banging into rocks. And once he got there, he could burst into that damn cabin and take out two people before they could react. They wouldn't be expecting him at all.

And he had been a pretty good marksman even before the Army and he'd kept it up with all the hunting trips and target practice.

He *liked* shooting. A target range was one of his favorite places to spend time.

Or it had been before he'd killed a man.

His alternatives had become so narrow since Will and Karl had told him to kill a man or be killed himself. He could go to the police, turn himself in.

Yeah. And if he pointed a finger at those two, which he increasingly wanted to do, they'd have each other for alibis. Friends? Friends? Really? He couldn't think of them that way anymore. He'd told them he'd keep his mouth shut, but they'd threatened him anyway.

Psychopaths.

After the way Will had talked to him tonight, he was beginning to wonder if they wouldn't kill him anyway even if he got rid of Blaire Afton.

He swore loudly. There was no one to hear, so why not? He needed to vent the horrible stew of overwhelming anger, hatred, fear and self-loathing he was now living in. Thanks to Will and Karl.

His friends. Lifelong friends. Why had he never before noticed they were missing something essential? That thing that made most people humane: compassion.

How could he have missed that they were basically ice inside and only pretended to be like everyone else?

Well, he'd missed it until just recently, and now he was paying for his blindness. Kinda astonishing that he could know someone for so long and not see the rot at their core.

Now there was rot at his, as well. When this was over, he swore to himself, he would never again speak to either of them. Never. He would banish them from his life and try to find some way to make up for the ugliness that had planted inside him.

But first he had to get through this, and if he was going to get through this, he needed to act soon or there'd never be any atonement.

He shook his head sharply, trying to get rid of the thought. Atonement? Later. Because right now he wasn't sure there could ever be any, even if he spent the rest of his life trying.

He was a wimp. Will had called him that and he was right. If he weren't such a wimp, he'd have put the gun to his own head.

But then, unbidden, came thoughts of his wife and soon-to-be-born child. He'd managed not to think of them once through this whole mess, managed to keep them separate and clean, and prevent their memories from making him feel any uglier than he already did.

Now they surged to the forefront, and one question froze even his shivering from the cold. How in the hell could he ever touch Dinah again with these soiled hands?

IN THE CABIN, the lattes were almost drained from their tall cups. Gus had drawn Blaire close to his side and kept an arm around her while they sipped and watched the fire dance.

"We'll go out again tomorrow," he told her. "If there's anything left to be found, we'll find it."

She wanted to believe him, but she knew she had to look, unlikely though it was. She wouldn't rest unless she tried. That was how she was built.

"Promise you won't hate me?" he said a few minutes later.

"I don't think I could do that," she said honestly. He'd been there every time she'd needed him for an emotional crisis in the last couple of years. Every time she'd needed him for anything.

"Oh," he answered, "it's always possible."

She shook her head a little. "Why are you afraid I'd hate you?"

"Because I want to cross a line."

She caught her breath as her heart slammed into a faster rhythm. "Gus?" she nearly whispered.

"I want to kiss you," he said quietly but bluntly. "I'm going out of my mind wanting you. I realize you probably don't feel the same but..."

"Hush," she said, hardly able to keep her breath.

He hushed instantly and started to draw his arm away. That was not at all what she wanted. She twisted around until she was pressed into him and able to look straight at his face.

"Kiss me. Just do it. And don't stop there."

She watched his expression change radically. It went from a little intense to soft warmth. "Blaire, I wasn't..."

"No, but I am. I know I've been trying to hide my attraction to you because I didn't want to damage our friendship, but—" She stopped, all of a sudden afraid that she'd gone way too far, that he might want to get out of here without even that kiss he'd asked for.

Then he spoke, hardly more than a murmur. "I was worried about the same thing. What we have is already irreplaceable."

She nodded, her mouth going dry, her throat threatening to close off and her heart hammering hard enough to leap out of her breast. She'd blown it, and she hadn't been this frightened since her first exposure to hostile fire. "We can keep it," she said hoarsely and hopefully. "We're grown-ups."

"I want a lot more than a kiss from you," he said. "A lot. But if you change your mind..."

"I know how to say no. I'm not saying it."

He started to smile, but before the expression completed, he clamped his mouth over hers in the most commanding, demanding kiss she'd ever felt. Her heart soared as his tongue slipped past her lips and began to plunder her mouth in a timeless rhythm.

Electric sparkles joined the mayhem he'd already set loose in her, filling her with heat and desire and a longing so strong it almost made her ache.

She'd waited forever, and now the wait was over. He was claiming her in the only way she'd ever wanted to be claimed.

She raised a hand, clutching at his shirt, hanging on to him for dear life. This felt so right, so good. So perfect. *Never let it end.* Then she felt his hand begin to caress her, first down her side, then slipping around front until he cradled her breast.

His touch was gentle, almost respectful, as he began to knead sensitive flesh through layers of sweater, shirt and bra. Those layers might as well have not been there. The thrill from his touch raced through her body all the way to her center until she had to clamp her thighs together. She felt her nipple harden, and when he drew back slightly from the kiss she had to gasp for air.

"You're so beautiful," he whispered, releasing her breast just long enough to brush her hair back from her cheek. "Beautiful. I've had to fight to keep my hands off you."

Music to her soul. When he released her she almost cried out, but he stood and drew her up with him. Then she looked down as he pushed the cardigan off her shoulders and reached for the buttons of her work shirt. She wished she were wearing lace and satin, fancy lingerie, instead of simple cotton, but the wish vanished swiftly as he pushed the shirt off her shoulders and let it fall to the floor.

His gaze drank her in, noting her in a way that made her feel as if he truly never wanted to forget a single line of her. Then with a twist, he released the back clasp of her bra and it, too, drifted to the floor as she spilled free of her confinement.

"Perfect," he muttered, bending his head to suck one of her nipples.

She gasped again as the electric charge ran through her and set off an ache at her center that could be answered only one way. Helplessly she grabbed his head, holding him close, never wanting the sensation to end.

She felt his fingers working the button of her jeans, then his hands pushing them down along with her undies. Then, taking his mouth from her breast, causing her to groan a protest, he urged her back onto the couch.

Her eyes, which had closed at some point she couldn't remember, opened a bit to see him tug her pants off and toss them away. Then without a moment's hesitation he began to strip himself, baring to her hungry gaze the hard lines of a male body at its peak of perfection.

"You're gorgeous," she croaked as he un-wrapped himself.

"Not as gorgeous as you," he said huskily.

Man, he was ready for her, and her insides quivered and clenched in recognition. All of him was big, and right now all of him was hard, too.

He reached for her hands and pulled her up until she was pressed against him, front to front, and his powerful arms wrapped around her. As he bent his head to drop kisses on her neck, she shivered with delight and with being naked against his heated nakedness.

There was no feeling in the world, she thought, like skin on skin, like having his hard, satiny member pressed against the flat of her belly, an incitement and a promise.

"Want to go up to the loft or make a pallet down here?" he asked her between kisses.

She sighed, hanging on to her mind with difficulty while he busily tried to strip her to basic instincts. "Climbing that ladder isn't sexy."

"Unless you're the one climbing behind."

Her sleepy eyes popped all the way open as she felt as if she were drowning in the gray pools of his. They wrapped around her like his arms, the color of the stormy sky outside, but bringing a storm of a very different kind. And with them came a sleepy smile.

Teasing her. At a time like this. She loved it as warmth continued to spread into her and turn into heat like lava. Her legs began to quiver, and all she wanted was to feel his weight atop her and his member hard inside her.

He must have felt her starting to slip, because suddenly his hands cupped her rump, such an exquisite and intimate experience, and lifted her. Then he put her carefully on the couch.

"Before one of us falls down," he said thickly, "I'll make that pallet."

Damn, she hated that he'd let her go, but there was nothing she could do except press her legs together in anticipation, waiting for the moment he would satisfy the burgeoning ache inside her.

He grabbed the folded blankets she had given him the night before and spread them on the rug before the hearth, folding them in half for extra padding. The pillow soon joined it. Then before she could stir much at all, he once again lifted her and laid her down on the bed he'd made for the two of them.

Softness below, hardness above, heat from one

side and a chill from the other. Sensations overwhelmed her, each seeming to join and augment the hunger he had awakened in her. "Gus..." she whispered, at once feeling weak and yet so strong. Her hands found his powerful shoulders, clinging. Her legs parted, inviting his possession.

Nobody in her life had ever made her feel this hot so swiftly. No one. It was as if he possessed a magic connection to all the nerve endings in her body, so that his least touch made every single one of them tingle with awareness and need.

He kissed her mouth again, deeply but more gently. His hands wandered her shoulders, her neck, and then her breasts. After a few minutes of driving her nearly crazy with longing, his mouth latched onto her nipple, sucking strongly until she arched with each pull of his mouth, feeling devoured but hungrier still. Her hips bucked in response, finding her rhythm, and then, depriving her of breath, he entered her.

Filled, stretched and finding the answer she had so needed, she stilled for just a moment, needing to savor him, needing the moment to last forever.

He must have felt nearly the same, because he, too, stilled, then caught her face between his hands. Her eyelids fluttered and she looked into his eyes, feeling as if she could see all the way to his soul.

Never had any moment felt so exquisite.

HUNGER WASHED THROUGH Gus in powerful waves. He'd had good sex before, but this was beyond any previous experience. Something about Blaire had lit rockets in him, driving him in ways that stole his self-control.

Part of his mind wanted to make this flawless, to give her every possible sensation he could before completion. Most of him refused to listen. There'd be another time for slow exploration, gentle touches and caresses. Time to learn all that delighted her.

Right now he could not ignore the one goal his body drove toward. After those moments of stillness that had seemed to come from somewhere out among the stars, his body took over again, leaving his brain far behind.

A rocket to the moon. A journey beyond the solar system. A careening sense of falling into the center of the universe.

Everything that mattered was here and now. All of it. Blaire and he became the sole occupants in a special world beyond which nothing else existed.

He pumped into her, hearing her gasps, moans and cries, goaded by them and by the way her hips rose to meet his. Her nails dug into his shoulders, the pain so much a part of the pleasure that they were indistinguishable.

He felt culmination overtake her, felt it in the stiffening of her body and the keening cry that escaped her. He held on to the last shred of his self-control until he heard her reach the peak once more.

Then he jetted into her, into the cosmos. Into a place out of time and mind, feeling as if his entire soul spilled into her.

EVENTUALLY HE CAME BACK to their place in time, aware that he had collapsed on her, that his weight might be uncomfortable. But she was still clinging to his shoulders, and when he tried to roll off she made a small sound of protest, trying to hang on, then let him go.

"My God," he whispered.

"Yeah," she murmured in reply.

Perspiration dried quickly in the heat from the fire. He rolled over and draped an arm around her waist. "You okay?"

"Okay? I don't think I've ever been better."

He saw her smile dawn on her puffy lips. He'd kissed her too hard, but at least she wasn't wincing. That kiss had come from deep within him, expressing a desire he'd been trying to bury since he'd first met her.

But since she wasn't complaining, he wasn't going to apologize. She wiggled around a bit until she faced him and placed her hand on his chest. "We can do this again, right?"

If he hadn't spent every ounce of energy he

had on her, he'd have laughed and proved it. Instead he returned her smile and said, "Believe it."

She closed her eyes, still smiling, and ran her palm over his smooth skin. "All this time and I never dreamed how perfect you are without clothing."

"Perfect? You're missing the scars."

"Battle scars," she retorted. "I have a few, too. You didn't point them out and I'm blind to yours. Just take the heartfelt compliment. I knew you were in great shape, I just never imagined such a striking package."

"I can say the same. I've been pining for you since day one."

A quiet little laugh escaped her. "We were behaving."

"We wanted to take care of our friendship."

Her eyes opened wider. "I know. Have we blown it?"

He shook his head slowly. "I don't think so."

"Me, either. This feels incredibly right."

He thought so, too. Holding her close was no longer ruled by the passion between them. He felt a different kind of warmth growing in him, the sense that an emptiness had been filled, that places perennially cold in his heart were thawing. He gave himself up to the gift that felt perilously close to a peace he had forgotten existed.

He was not the kind of man who wished for the impossible, but at that moment he wished he could stay in this place forever, with Blaire in his arms, with the warmth in his heart and soul. To cling to feelings he'd lost so long ago, that had become the detritus of war.

He spent a lot of time *not* thinking about the war. Sometimes it was like trying to avoid the elephant in the room, but he tried to focus on the present day and the needs of the forest he protected and the people he served. Just taking care of Mother Nature and offering a bandage to a kid who'd cut his finger on a sharp piece of wood, those things made him feel good about himself.

So he tried not to remember. Still, the demons roared up out of the depths from time to time. They did for Blaire, too, and when it happened they got together whether in town for a trip to the diner or at one of their headquarters. Sometimes they hardly had to speak at all. A simple word or two would convey everything that was necessary.

They'd been balm for each other for a long time. He actually depended on her and she seemed to depend on him. But this was so very different. This wasn't dependence of any kind. This was a meeting of two souls with a hunger for something greater.

She ran her hand over his back, not paying any special attention to the burn scar that wrinkled his back on one side. "Your skin feels so good," she murmured.

He stroked her side in return. "So does yours. Plus your curves. Enough to drive a guy crazy. Did that give you any trouble on duty?" He'd seen more than enough men crossing the line with women in their units.

"Some. Funny thing, though. After infantry training I wasn't an easy target anymore. Most of them wisely didn't press the issue."

He liked the thought of her scaring the bejesus out of some young fool who thought he was entitled to take what he wanted, to expect some woman to be grateful for his attentions.

"I was also luckier than some because my superiors weren't into sexual harassment at all."

"Fortunate. I saw some of that stuff. I'm glad it overlooked you."

And there they were, returning to the safe—safe?—ground of their military experience. He could have sighed, and it was all his fault.

Then he found the escape hatch before he totally destroyed the mood. His stomach growled. A giggle escaped Blaire.

"Yeah," he said. "I guess the soup didn't stick. Want me to wander into the kitchen and find something for both of us?"

IN THE END, they slipped into jeans and shirts and went barefoot into the kitchen together. She did have a few things handy, things she didn't usually buy in any kind of quantity because they were too tempting. But tucked into her freezer, lying flat beneath a load of other food, was a frozen pizza.

"I can doctor it with canned mushrooms and some fresh bell peppers," she offered. She'd splurged on a couple of peppers at the store. In fact, as she looked inside her fridge, she saw a whole bunch of splurges she'd hardly been aware of making. Her mood? Or because she had hoped that Gus would stay the night again? The latter, she suspected. Regardless, her usually bare refrigerator was stuffed to the gills tonight.

"Mind if I look around?"

She waved him toward the fridge. "Help yourself. And if you like to cook, so much the better."

But cooking never became involved. He found her brick of white Vermont cheddar cheese, an unopened package of pepperoni slices that she'd almost forgotten she had and a box of wheat crackers in the cupboard. He wielded her chef's knife like a pro and soon had a large plate full of sliced, crumbly cheese with crackers and pepperoni. It looked like a professional job.

"I suppose I should have saved the pepperoni for the pizza," he said as he carried the plate into the living room and pulled the end table around to hold it. She followed with two cans of cola.

"That pizza is a desperation measure," she answered. "I can always get more pepperoni."

They curled up on the couch together. She tucked her legs beneath herself.

These moments were heavenly, she thought as she nibbled on crackers and cheese. Everything felt so right. She only wished it could last. And it might, for the rest of the night.

But her PTSD was still gnawing at the edges of her mind, trying to warn her of the threat outside, a threat held at bay only by the violent storm.

Except she couldn't be certain there was any threat at all. Just leftover tatters of her mind from some seriously bad experience.

She tried to shake it off and let her head lean against Gus's shoulder. He didn't seem to mind at all. Every so often he passed her a cracker holding a bit of cheese or pepperoni. Taking care of her.

A sudden loud crack of thunder, sounding as if it were right in the room, caused her to start. The bolt of lightning flashed even through the curtains that were closed against the night.

"Wow," she murmured. It awoke memories she didn't want, causing her to leave the comfort of being close to Gus. She rose and began to pace rapidly, wishing the room were a lot bigger.

"Blaire?"

She glanced at him, taking in his frown, but she suspected he knew exactly what was going on. That crack of thunder had sounded like weapons fire. Too loud, too close. Her hands suddenly itched to be holding her rifle, her body to be ducking down behind something until she could locate the threat.

At least she didn't try to hide. She hadn't lost her sense of where she *really* was, but the sound had awakened deeply ingrained impulses. At least there'd been only one crack of thunder. The grumbling continued, but that's all it was, grumbling.

"It was just thunder," Gus said.

But she could tell he was reminding himself as much as her. Some things, she thought, would never be normal again. She hated the fireworks displays the town put on, so she stayed out here rather than joining the celebration. At least fireworks were forbidden in the state park and in the national forest.

Which, of course, didn't mean she never had to put a stop to them and threaten people with arrest if they didn't listen. But walking up to a campsite where people were setting off bottle rockets, reminiscent of the sound of mortars, and firecrackers that sounded like gunshots... That was an effort of will on her part.

"Yeah," she answered Gus.

"I'd pace along with you but I think we'd collide."

"I'm sorry."

"Don't be. It jolted me, too. I'd been out about

six months when a kid lit a string of fireworks right behind me. Firecrackers, probably. I swung around instantly into a crouch and I really didn't see him. Didn't see the fireworks. I hate to think what might have happened if my buddy hadn't been there to call me back."

She nodded, understanding completely. Gradually the tension the bolt had set off in her was easing, and after a couple of more minutes she was able to return to the couch. She sat near him, but not right beside him. She didn't think she was ready to be touched yet.

He still held the plate of crackers and cheese that they'd made only a moderate dent on. "Have some more," he said, holding it toward her. "Eating something usually brings me back to the present. Especially something I never had overseas."

The fire had begun to burn down and she considered whether to put another log on it. Mundane thoughts. Safe thoughts. Her taste buds were indeed bringing her back from the cliff edge. Tart cheese, crunchy, slightly bitter wheat crackers. An anchor to the present moment.

At last she was able to look at Gus and smile. The magic of the evening was beginning to return.

JEFF GAVE UP. He didn't care if someone spotted him. He popped open a can of paraffin used to heat foods on the trail and lit the flame with his lighter. Then he set it in front of him, holding his freezing hands over it. Within minutes the survival blanket caught some of the flame's heat and began to reflect it back toward his face.

Thank God. He'd begun to think his nose would fall off from frostbite, although he was sure it wasn't *that* cold. Having to sit out here like this was pure misery, and he wondered that he hadn't started shivering. Although his insulated rain jacket was probably capturing his body heat as effectively as it kept the rain out.

As soon as his fingers felt a little better, he reached inside his jacket and pulled out a pack of cigarettes from his breast pocket. They were a little crushed, but still smokable, and damn he needed a smoke.

The misery of the night was beginning to drive him past moral considerations. He hated his friends even more now, but step by step he made up his mind to get Blaire Afton out of the way so he never needed to do this again.

One shot. He was pretty good at several hundred yards. Maybe more. That other ranger wouldn't be able to find him fast enough if he picked his spot and knew all the places for concealment or quick escape. First thing in the morning, he promised himself. Then he was going to shoot Blaire in the same way he would shoot a game animal.

After that, having bought a few days, he was going to move to Timbuktu or some other far-away place so that Will and Karl would leave him alone. Forever. He just wanted to be left alone forever. Dinah and his baby would be better off without him. Yeah, he could run as far as he wanted.

And he didn't care if it was called running because, damn it, he needed to run for his life. He no longer trusted those guys not to kill him anyway. They weren't going to let him go simply because he'd done what he'd been told to do.

Then another thought crept into his brain. Why shoot Blaire if it wasn't going to save his own life?

Double damn, he thought. Why had he needed to think of that? Because, he reminded himself, killing her would give him time to make plans and extricate himself. He couldn't just march out of here tomorrow and be on a plane by midnight. Nothing was that easy, even without thinking of his family.

He started making a mental list as he continued to warm his hands. Passport. Cash. Arranging for his bank and credit cards to accept charges from overseas. Clothes. He needed to take at least some clothing with him. He wasn't rich like the other two and couldn't be needlessly wasteful.

But he *did* have enough to get away to some

cheaper place, and enough to sustain him until he could find some kind of work. He didn't mind getting his hands dirty, he was strong and healthy, and educated. He ought to be able to find something somewhere.

Regardless, he figured if he left the country, Will and Karl would lose all interest in him. He wouldn't be around to make them nervous, or to annoy them. Out of sight, out of mind would most likely apply because he didn't think either one of them would want to waste time tracking him down in some other country.

Yeah. Kill the woman and hightail it. The plan would work. He just needed to take care the other ranger couldn't find him first. Hell, he ought to shoot the man, as well. Will had suggested it. It would certainly buy him time to leave this park behind, to get out of the mountains.

Another thing to hash over in his mind as he sat there in misery. He hardly even noticed that the storm rolled out after midnight. All *that* did was make the night colder.

Damn, his life sucked.

Chapter Eleven

Blaire and Gus made their way up to her loft
bedroom instead of feeding the fire on the stone
hearth. Heat rose and it had filled the loft, which
captured it. Blaire's predecessor had used the
room farthest back in this cabin for a bedroom,
but it hadn't taken long for Blaire to figure out
the loft stayed warmer on frigid winter nights.
She burned less fuel and didn't need to use space
heaters. She now used the back room for storage.

Her successor would probably change everything around, a thought that occasionally amused
her. As it was, she had a tidy space, big enough
for a queen bed, a small chest of drawers, a night
table, a chair and a lamp. Inconvenient as far as
needing a bathroom, but it was a small price to
pay.

She had to warn Gus to watch out for his head,
though. The loft ceiling nearly scraped her head.

"This is cozy," he remarked. The light had

several settings and she had turned it on low so he was cast in a golden glow.

"*Cozy* is a pleasant word for *tiny*," she answered. "But I like it."

"I can see why. Nice and warm, too."

Three or four minutes later they were both tucked under her comforter, naked and locked in tight embrace.

This time Gus used his mouth and tongue to explore her, at one point disappearing beneath the covers to kiss and lick her sweet center until she thought she was going to lose her mind. When she was sure she couldn't stand it anymore, she turned the tables, rising over him to discover his defined muscles, the hollows between them and finally the silky skin of his erection. It jumped at her first touch, and she felt an incredible sense of power and pleasure, unlike anything she'd ever felt.

But he was doing a lot of that to her, giving her new sensations and a new appreciation of sex. This was in no way the mundane experience she'd had in the past. This was waking her to an entirely new view of being a woman.

She enjoyed his every moan and shudder as her tongue tried to give him the same pleasures he had shared with her earlier. Finally his hands caught her shoulders and pulled her up. Straddling his hips, she took him inside her, then rested on him, feeling as if they truly became one.

Their hips, welded together, moved together, and the rising tide of passion swept her up until it carried her away almost violently. They reached the peak together, both of them crying out simultaneously.

Then, feeling as if she floated on the softest cloud, Blaire closed her eyes and drifted away.

LYING LIKE SPOONS beneath the covers, Gus cradled her from behind, holding her intimately. She felt his warm breath against the back of her ear, and even as sleep tried to tug at her, she spoke.

"That was heaven."

"If that was heaven, sign me up." Then he gave a whispery laugh. "I'm sure it was better."

She smiled into the dark in response. "I don't think I've ever felt this good."

"Me, either." He pressed a kiss to her cheek, then settled back again. Their heads shared the same pillow and she could feel his every move. "I hate to be the practical one, but the storm has passed and if you want to ride out in the morning..."

She sighed. "We need to sleep. I know. I've been fighting it off because I don't want to miss a minute of this."

"This won't be the last minute," he answered. "Unless you tell me to take a hike, I plan on being right here with you tomorrow night."

She hesitated. "What about Holly?"

"She always wanted to replace me."

Blaire gasped. "Seriously?"

He chuckled. "Not really. But she enjoys ruling the roost sometimes. Which is the only reason I can ever take a vacation or get to town. Holly is the best, but she's told me more than once that she likes being able to point at me when someone's unhappy."

"Ooh, not so nice." She was teasing and she could tell he knew it when he laughed.

"She has her moments, all right." She felt him pull her a little closer. "Sleep," he said. "It's going to be a long day in the saddle."

IN THE EARLY morning, before the sun had risen when the light was still gray, Gus went to the corral out back to check on the horses. They regarded him almost sleepily and stood close together because the chill had deepened overnight. Remembering summers elsewhere, he sometimes wondered how folks could ever really think of this climate as having a summer. A few hot days, but up here in the forest on the mountain little of that heat reached them. Eighty degrees was a heat wave.

The lean-to over one part of the corral, against the cabin, seemed to have done its job. The wind must have been blowing from a different direction because the feed was dry and if the horses had gotten wet at all, he couldn't tell. Even their blankets seemed mostly dry.

They nickered at him, apparently glad to see a human face. He could well imagine. The night's rain had left a lot of mud behind, and that wasn't good for them to stand in. He needed to move them out of here soon.

He loved the morning scents of the woods after a storm, though. The loamy scent of the forest floor, the pines seeming to exhale their aroma with delight…all of it. Fresh, clean and unsullied by anything else.

Well, except horse poop, he corrected himself with amusement. Grabbing a shovel that leaned against the cabin wall, he scooped up as much as he could find and dumped it into the compost pile on the other side of the fence. He wondered if the compost ever got put to use. He knew some folks came up to grab a load or two of his in the spring for their backyard gardens. Maybe they came here, too. He turned some of it and felt the heat rise. Good. It was aging.

Smelly, though, he thought with amusement. So much for that fresh morning aroma.

The sky had lightened a little more as he returned inside, wondering if he should start breakfast or let Blaire sleep. He was used to running on only a couple of hours of sleep in the field. Today wouldn't be a problem for him. He didn't know about her.

As he stepped inside, he smelled bacon. Well, that answered the question. He passed the kitchen area to the bathroom, where he washed his hands, then returned to Blaire.

"Morning," he said. "I hope I didn't wake you when I got up."

"Not really. I was starting to stir. How are the horses?"

"Champs. They're fine, but they really need a ride today. At the moment they're standing in mud."

She turned from the stove to look at him and he thought he saw a slight pinkening of her cheeks. "Bad for them?"

"Bad for their hooves if they stand too long. A few hours won't cause a problem, I'm sure, but I know they'd feel better if they could dry off their feet."

"Who wouldn't?" She turned back to the stove and flipped some strips of bacon.

"Can I help?"

"Make some toast if you want it. We've got power this morning, amazingly enough. I was sure that storm would have left us blacked out. Anyway, the toaster's over there. We don't have to use the flame on the stove."

He found a loaf of wheat bread next to the toaster and a butter dish with a full stick. He dug out a knife and began by popping two slices of bread into the toaster. "Did you ever see those four-sided metal tents you could use to make toast over a gas flame?"

She thought a moment. "Those things with the little wooden handles so you could pull down the piece that held the bread in place against the grill? My great-grandmother had one, but I never saw her use it."

"I've sometimes thought I'd like to find one somewhere. Power goes out over at my place, too, and I like my toast."

"Then we ought to look for one. Now that you mention it, that would probably help me out a lot in the winter."

He watched her fork bacon onto a plate with a paper towel on it. She immediately placed more strips in the pan. "I stuck my nose outside," she said. "It's cold, isn't it?"

"Relatively. We'll need jackets and gloves for certain."

"Then we should eat hearty. Stoke the internal heater."

He absolutely didn't have any problem with that.

THEY RODE OUT after the sun crested the mountains far to the east. It hung red and hazy for a while, then brightened to orange. Soon it became too brilliant to look at.

The cold clung beneath the trees, however. At

Gus's suggestion they started circling the murder scene about two hundred yards out.

"He had to watch for a while before moving in," Gus said needlessly as they had already discussed this. "So he'd have some kind of hide. Maybe use one left by another hunter."

She was riding beside him as their path through the trees allowed it. A slight shudder escaped her. "I don't like the way you phrased that. *Another* hunter. Like this guy was after deer or elk."

She had a point. "I hope you know I didn't mean it that way."

"I do," she acknowledged.

"You okay?"

"Hell, no," she answered frankly. "Ants of bad memories are crawling up and down my spine, and occasionally all over me. If you mowed this forest to the ground, maybe then I'd be able to believe there isn't an ambush out here waiting for us."

"I read you." Yeah, he did. It might all be PTSD from their time in war, but whether it was didn't matter. They couldn't afford to ignore it until they were *sure* the shooter wasn't out here.

A little farther along, she spoke again. "We started this whole idea to find evidence."

"True."

"How much could be left after that storm last night? Seriously."

He shook his head but refused to give in to the despair that sometimes accompanied the memories. His brain had a kink in it since Afghanistan and all he could do was make the best use of it he might. Ignoring it never won the day.

They used both GPS and a regular compass to navigate their way around a wide arc. The GPS didn't always catch a weak satellite signal through the trees, but as soon as another satellite was in place it would strengthen. In the interim, when the signal failed, they used the old-fashioned method.

About an hour later, Blaire made a sound of disgust. "I haven't yet been able to see the Jasper tent through the trees. If someone was going to observe, he'd need the sight line or he'd have to be a lot closer. What's the smart money?"

Gus reined in Scrappy and waited until Blaire came fully beside him, their legs almost touching.

"Here." He reached into his saddlebag and pulled out a huge pair of binoculars that would have served a sniper's crew well. "Look upslope and see what catches your attention."

"Why up?"

"Because if there's a high spot up there, or even along this arc, those trees aren't necessarily going to matter. We don't have to see *through* them."

She gave him a crooked smile. "Which is why

you were special ops and I wasn't." She looked upslope again. "You're right, I'm probably looking in the wrong direction."

"We should look both ways. In case he might have found an open sight line here, too."

"I hope we're not on a fool's errand," she remarked as they moved forward.

"We've got to look. Neither of us is the type to sit on our hands." Nor did he want to tell her that he could swear he felt eyes boring into the back of his neck. Those sensations had never let him down in the 'Stan, but they hadn't always been right, either.

Even so... "You know, Blaire, we're both concerned he's still hanging around, but I can't understand why he would."

"I can't understand why he killed that poor man in the first place. Besides, I've heard criminals like to come back to the scene. To relive their big moment. To see what the cops are doing. We're looking. Maybe he's interested in that. Maybe it makes him feel important."

"Possibly." He tilted his head a little, looking at his display and seeing the GPS was down again. He pulled the compass out of his breast pocket to make sure they were still following their planned route. So far so good. He looked downslope again but saw only trees. A lot of trees. He could have sighed. "That was good reasoning, you know."

She had been looking upslope with the binoculars. "What was?"

He smiled. "Your rationale for why he still might be here. Maybe our senses are completely off-kilter."

She lowered her head for a moment, then said something that made his heart hurt. "I hope not. I'm still learning to trust my perceptions again."

THEY WERE GETTING too close, Jeff thought. He'd made his way back to the hide atop a big boulder from which he'd watched the campground. It would give some hunter a panorama for tracking game. For him it gave a view of the killing field.

He caught himself. That was too dramatic. That called to mind the most god-awful massacre, and he didn't want to associate with that, even in a private moment of thought.

But putting his binoculars to his eyes, he watched the two of them. If he took Blaire out now, the guy might dismount to take care of her. Would he have time to get away before the man came looking for him?

He looked up the slope and recalled the night of the shooting. He'd had to go into the campground that night, right to the tent. This time he could keep a much safer distance and just hightail it. It wasn't as far, and he knew the way. He ought to since he'd covered the path so many times.

Shooting Blaire might spook the horses, too. The guy—Gus, he thought—might get thrown. That would be helpful. Of course, a man could probably run faster over this terrain than a horse could. But would he leave Blaire if she was bleeding?

Yeah, if she was already dead.

Crap.

He rolled over again and watched the two of them. If they came up any higher, he was going to have to retreat from this spot. He had little doubt they'd find it. It worked as a deer blind, not a human blind. The guy who'd built this nest hadn't wanted it to be impossible to find in subsequent years. Too much work had gone into it, such as moving heavy rocks for a base.

Damn, he wanted a cigarette. The thought made him look down and he realized he'd left a heap of butts already. Damn! He scooped them up and began to stuff them into a pocket. Not enough to leave a shell casing behind. No, now he'd leave DNA for sure. Maybe Will was right to scorn him.

No, Will wasn't right. Will wasn't right about a damn thing except he needed to make sure Blaire didn't have a sudden memory of him and make a connection.

Then Jeff was going to clear his butt out of this country.

His thoughts stuttered a bit and he wondered

if his thinking was getting screwed up. Energy bars barely staved off the cold and he was almost out of them. Maybe his brain was skipping important things.

But he knew one thing for sure. If he went back without killing that woman, Will and Karl were going to kill *him*. So he had to do it. Just to buy time.

He needed those two to split up a little more. More space between them, more distance. He didn't want to add *two* people to a body count that shouldn't even exist.

He closed his eyes briefly, wishing himself on another planet. Or even dead and buried. Anything but lying here watching a woman he had nothing against, waiting for an opportunity to shoot her as if she were a game animal.

It was self-defense, he told himself. Indirectly, perhaps, but he needed to defend himself and this was the only way. Self-defense. He kept repeating it like a mantra.

GUS DREW REIN and Scrappy slowed, then stopped. Realizing it, Blaire slowed Lita down and looked over at him. "Something wrong?"

"Scrappy just started to limp. Maybe he's got a loose shoe or something. I need to check. Give me a minute?"

"Of course." She watched him dismount, then turned her attention to the woods around them.

She just didn't see any place yet that would have given the shooter a clear view of the campground. They needed to get higher, unless Scrappy was truly lame, in which case they'd have to head back.

Because she was busy telling herself this was a fool's errand, they'd never find anything useful and it was simply born of their military training that required them to act against a threat… Well, she wouldn't necessarily mind if they had to call this off. She loved being out here on horseback, and Lita was a great mount, but the sense of danger lurking around every tree was ruining it and probably ridiculous besides.

Since she'd left the combat zone for the last time, she'd been forced to realize how powerful post-traumatic stress could be. She hadn't been inflicted with it as badly as some of her former comrades, but she had it. Enough to make her uneasy for no damn good reason, like the last few days.

A random murder had occurred. It might not even be random at all. They wouldn't know that until the police collected more evidence. But right now, riding through the woods, hoping to find the place from which the shooter could have observed the campground, had its footing more in her memories than in the present.

Yeah, it was creepy, but *this* creepy? She needed to talk herself down. Needed to accept that the killer was long gone and every bit of the uneasiness she couldn't shake was being internally generated by a heap of bad memories that couldn't quite be buried.

Then maybe she could get back to doing her job, and Gus could get back to doing his. Holly and Dave might not mind standing in for them for a while, but it wasn't fair. They both had jobs to do and they were letting them slide because neither of them could quite believe in the safety of the woods.

That thought caused her to sit back in the saddle. Couldn't believe in the safety of the woods? Seriously? This retreat she had come to in order to escape the bustle of the busy, populated world because it somehow grated on her and kept her on alert too much? It no longer felt safe?

God, this was bad. Maybe she needed to get some counseling. Never had the detritus of her military experience gotten this far out of hand. Nightmares, yeah. Disliking crowds, yeah. But the woods? The safe haven she'd found here?

"It seems he got a stone in his hoof," Gus said, dropping Scrappy's right foreleg to the ground.

"Do we need to go back?"

"Nah. I've got a tool in my saddlebag. I'll get it out in a minute and then we can move on."

She watched him come around Scrappy's left side and unbuckle the saddlebag. "Is he bruised?"

"I don't know yet. He didn't limp for long, so I hope not."

"Well...if he needs a rest..." She trailed off as it hit her how far away they were now from everything. Miles from her cabin. Probably miles from the dirt road. Could they shortcut it through the woods? Maybe. It all depended on how many ravines were lurking between here and there. So far they'd been lucky. At any moment the mountain could throw up a huge stop sign.

"It'll be fine," Gus said as he pulled out the tool. "We can always walk them, but I don't think it'll be necessary."

Blaire felt the punch before she heard the report. She started to fall sideways and grabbed the saddle horn only to feel it slip from her fingers. She felt another blow, this one to her head as she wondered with confusion why she was on the ground. Then everything went black.

JEFF HAD A clear escape route. He could run up to the cave like a mountain goat, nothing in his way from here. When the guy dismounted his horse and started to check its hoof, it seemed like a fateful opportunity. He had a clear shot at Blaire, and from over two hundred yards he had no doubt he could make it.

If he was one thing, he was a superb marksman with this rifle. One shot was all he'd need.

He looked downslope and liked what he saw.

Damn fool ranger wouldn't be able to reach this spot fast. Too many rocks, a ravine that looked deep enough to swallow him and his horse. It made great protection for Jeff.

Okay, then.

Lifting his rifle to his shoulder, he pulled the bolt to put a shell in the chamber. Then, with his elbows resting on a rock, he looked through the scope. Suddenly Blaire was big, a huge target.

Holding his breath, steadying his hands until the view from the scope grew perfectly still, he fired. He waited just long enough to see Blaire fall from her horse.

Then he grabbed his pack and gun and started to run uphill. He didn't wait to see the result. He didn't need to. He was a damn fine shot.

What he hadn't seen was that the man was looking right in his direction when he fired.

Gus removed the stone from Scrappy's foot and tossed it away. Bending, he looked closely and saw nothing worrisome. He straightened and looked up at Blaire, who was still straddling Lita. "He might be a bit tender later, but he's fine to continue."

"Good," she said.

Then the entire world shifted to slow motion. He saw a flash from up in the woods some distance away. His mind registered it as a muzzle flash. Only then did he hear the familiar *crack*.

Before he could act, he saw red spread across Blaire's sleeve and begin to drip on her hand. He had to get her down. *Now.*

She reached for the saddle horn, but before he could get there, she tipped sideways and fell off Lita. He heard the thud as her head hit the ground.

Everything inside him froze. The clearheaded state of battle washed over him, curling its ice around everything within him, focusing him as nothing else could.

He left Scrappy standing and dealt with Lita, who was disturbed enough by the sound and Blaire's tumble to be dancing nervously. He feared she might inadvertently trample Blaire as she lay on the ground, so he grabbed her by the bridle, then grabbed Scrappy with his other hand.

He knew horses well enough to know that Scrappy might react to Lita's nervousness and begin to behave the same way. While it wasn't usually necessary, he used the reins to tie Scrappy to a tree trunk along with Lita.

They nickered and huffed, an equine announcement of *let's get out of here*, but he was sure they weren't going anywhere.

Only then, what seemed like years later but couldn't have been more than a half minute, he knelt next to Blaire. She had the rag doll limpness he recognized as unconsciousness, and he feared how badly she might have hit her head.

But there was a sequence, and the first thing he needed to do was stanch the blood from her wound. Time slowed down until it dragged its heels. Only experience had taught him that was adrenaline speeding up his mind, that time still moved at its regular pace.

With adrenaline-powered strength, he ripped the sleeve of her jacket open and kept tearing until he could see where the blood was heaviest. Then he tore her shirt and revealed her shoulder, turning her partly over to see her back as well as her front.

A through-and-through wound, bleeding from both sides, but not through the artery, thank God. Bad enough, but no spurts. Grabbing the sleeve he had just torn, he ripped it in half and pushed it against the two holes, front and back, as hard as he could.

He could use her jacket sleeve for a tourniquet, he thought, but his mind was only partly on first aid. "Blaire. Blaire?"

Her unconsciousness worried him as much as anything. How hard had she hit her head? Head wounds could be the absolute worst, even though he was sure he could stop the bleeding from her shoulder.

He kept calling her name as he wound the jacket sleeve around her shoulder, making it tight. Stop the bleeding. Find a way to wake her up.

Only then could he search out the shooter, and he damn well knew where he was going to start.

BLAIRE CAME TO with a throbbing head and a shoulder that was throbbing even harder. She cussed and suddenly saw Gus's face above hers.

"Thank God," he said. "You hit your head."

"How long was I out and who shot me?"

"You were out for about two minutes and I don't know yet who shot you. But I saw the muzzle flash."

"Then go get him, Gus."

"No. I REALLY WANT to but I'm worried about you. I need to get you help."

She tried to sit up, wincing a bit, so he helped her, propping her against a tree.

"I don't think you lost a lot of blood," he said, "but if you start to get light-headed, you know what to do."

"Not my first rodeo," she said between her teeth. "The blow to my head wasn't that bad. I'm not seeing double or anything. The headache is already lessening. The shoulder... Well, it hurts like hell but I can't feel any serious damage." She moved her arm.

"The shooter messed up," she said after a few moments. "Just a flesh wound. He must have used a full metal jacket." Meaning that the bullet hadn't entered her shattering and spinning, causing a lot of internal damage.

"Blaire…"

She managed a faint smile. "I always wanted to say that."

He flashed a grin in response. "Your head is okay."

"My shoulder's not too bad, either."

He rested his hand on her uninjured shoulder, aware that time was ticking, both for her and for the escaping shooter. "I'm going to radio for help for you. Then, if you think you're okay by yourself for a bit, I'm going after that bastard."

With her good arm, she pushed herself up. "I'm coming with you."

"Stop. Don't be difficult, Blaire. You've been shot."

She caught his gaze with hers. "I've also been in combat. So have you. Trust me, I can judge my own fitness. There's a ravine up there and I know the way around it. What's more, he obviously has a long-range weapon. Do you? Do you really want to go after him alone? He could be perched anywhere."

He frowned at her, a frown that seemed to sink all the way to his soul. "You might start bleeding again."

"If I do, I'll tell you. This feels like you've got me bandaged pretty well. Quit frowning at me. I won't be stupid."

"Riding up there is stupid," he said flatly. But looking at her, he realized he was fighting a losing battle. If she could find a way to get herself back on Lita, she'd follow him. Never had he seen such a stubborn set to a woman's jaw. He wanted to throw up his hands in frustration. "I'm trained for this," he reminded her. "Solo missions."

"I'm trained, too," she retorted. With a shove, she reached her feet and remained steady. "See, I'm not even weak from blood loss. I'm *fine*."

Well, there were different definitions of that word, but he gave up arguing even though he had an urge to tie her to that tree. But, he understood, if that shooter realized she was still alive, he might be circling around right now. He could get in another shot without being seen.

"Hell and damnation," he growled. But he gave in. Better to keep her close.

He had to help her mount Lita since she had only one workable arm, but once she was astride the horse, feet in the stirrups, she looked fine. No paleness to her face, no sagging. Maybe the wound wasn't that awful.

It was her left shoulder that was injured and she was right-handed. Like many of the rangers out here who needed to go into the woods, she carried a shotgun as well as a pistol. The shotgun was settled into a holster in front of her right thigh, and before he would allow her to move, he asked her to prove she could pull it out and use it with one arm. She obliged while giving him an annoyed look.

"It's a shotgun," she said. "I hardly have to be accurate."

If he weren't getting hopping mad, he might have smiled. "I just need to be sure you can use it. And I'm radioing this in, like it or not. We aren't going to play solitary superheroes out here."

Damn! He'd gone from violent fear that she was dead into relief that she was reasonably okay and now he was so mad he was ready to kill.

Someone had shot her. Why? Hell, he didn't care why. Whoever it was, needed to be grabbed by the short and curlies, tied up in handcuffs and marched to jail.

As they moved farther upslope, his radio found an area with clear satellite transmission, and he gave the sheriff's office a rundown as they rode, including that Blaire had been wounded but was riding at his side. He asked they be tracked, and dispatch promised they would.

Insofar as possible, he thought as he hooked the radio onto his belt again. He kept glancing at Blaire to be sure she was still all right and wondered if she had any idea how distracting she was. This wasn't helping the search much. His concern for her wasn't making him a better hunter.

He would have liked to be able to shield her with his body, but since there was no way to know if the guy might circle around and take another shot, there was no safe place for her to ride. He suggested she lead the way because she knew how to get around the ravine, and all he had to do was point out where he had seen the muzzle flash. Plus, he could see if she started to weaken.

She was a born navigator with a lot of experience. She guided with surety, part of the trip taking them away from the area from which he'd seen the flash, much more of it angling toward it and up as they left the ravine behind.

He glanced down into that ravine as they crossed a narrow ledge of rock and realized there'd have been no way to cross it directly. None. The shooter was probably counting on it to slow them down.

But their horses moved swiftly when the terrain allowed. Soon they found a trampled muddy place that he'd probably been using. From there his trail was clear for about twenty feet or so, giving them direction, then it disappeared in the sopping duff and loam beneath the trees.

She drew rein and waited for him to catch up to her. "He probably followed as straight a path uphill as he could. For speed?"

He nodded. "I agree."

"And there's a road on the other side of that ridge," she said, pointing. "Not much of one, little more than a cart track used by hunters, but he could have left a vehicle there."

"I bet." He paused. "Let's speed up. This is a rough climb. He had to get winded. To slow down."

But the horses wouldn't, he thought. They'd just keep climbing steadily and as quickly as they could, as if they sensed the urgency. They probably did. Horses were sensitive animals.

He kept one eye on Blaire while he scanned the area around them. The guy might have angled away from a straight path. It all depended on how scared he was and how much time he thought he'd have. If the shooter thought Blaire was down, he might think he had a lot of time.

He hoped so. The fury in him had grown cold, a feeling he remembered from other conflicts. He was riding its wave, heedless of danger to himself, focused on the mission, focused on Blaire's safety. Nothing else mattered.

She, too, was scanning around them, but he had little hope they'd see much. The shooter probably had the sense to wear woodland camouflage, although the higher they climbed the thinner the trees grew. They were nowhere near the tree line, but for some reason the growth here was thinner. He tried to remember if there'd been a fire here at some point. The ground was plenty brushy, but the trees didn't seem as big or as stout as they had farther below.

Then he saw it. A flash of movement above them.

"Blaire."

She halted and looked back at him.

"I think I saw him. We're sitting ducks right now. We'd better split up." He hated to suggest it, given that she was wounded, probably suffering a great deal of pain and maybe even weakening. But together they made a great target.

"Where?" she asked quietly.

"Eleven o'clock. About three hundred yards upslope."

"Got it."

Then with a brief nod she turned Lita a bit, angling away from where he'd seen the movement. Misleading as if she were going to look elsewhere.

He did the same heading the other direction, but not too much, teeth clenched until his jaw screamed, hoping that their split wouldn't tell the guy they'd seen him.

Then Blaire called, "I think I saw something over here."

Did she want him to come her way? Or was she sending their intended misdirection up to the shooter?

"I'll be there in a minute," he called back. "Need room to turn around."

"Yo," she answered, her voice sounding a little fainter.

The brief conversation gave him the chance to look up again to the spot where he'd seen movement. There was more movement now. Rapid. Then something happened and he heard rocks falling. A man's shape, suddenly visible, lost its upward momentum and instead he seemed to be scrambling frantically.

Gotcha, he thought with burning satisfaction. "Now, Scrappy." He touched the horse with his heels, speeding him up. If ever he had needed this horse to be sure-footed, he needed it now. Scrappy didn't disappoint.

With amazing speed, the horse covered the ground toward the man, who was still struggling as more rocks tumbled on him from above. The guy had evidently made a serious misstep and gotten into a patch of very loose scree.

Taking it as a warning, Gus halted Scrappy about two hundred feet back, then dismounted, carrying his shotgun with him. He approached cautiously, aware that the guy was armed and desperate.

Then he swore as he saw Blaire emerge from the trees on the other side. He was hoping to have dealt with this before she entered the danger zone. He was, however, glad to see she'd unholstered her shotgun and angled Lita so she could use it.

"Keep a bead on him," Gus called to her as he hurried carefully toward the man.

The guy turned over, his rifle in his hands, looking as if he were ready to shoot. Gus instantly squatted and prepared to take aim, but the man evidently realized he was outnumbered. If he shot in any direction, one of two shotguns would fire at him.

"Put the rifle away," Gus demanded, rising and making it clear that he was ready to shoot. "Now."

He could see the guy's face clearly, reflecting panic. He looked around wildly, his feet pushing at the scree beneath him but gaining no purchase.

"Give up," Blaire called. "You wouldn't be the first man I've shot."

Well, that was blunt, Gus thought, easing closer to their quarry. Vets didn't like to say things like that. He hoped to hell that wasn't the blow to her head talking.

"I've got him," Gus called when he was ten feet away. Resignation had replaced panic on the guy's face. He took one hand from his rifle, and with the other tossed the weapon to the side.

Then he said the strangest thing: "I'm so glad I didn't kill her."

Chapter Twelve

A half hour later, with Jeff Walston securely bound in zip ties, Gus heard the sound of helicopter rotors from overhead. Medevac was on the way, and as he'd been told over the radio, a couple of cops were riding along.

Good. He needed to be away from the source of his anger. He had enough experience to know he wouldn't take it out on his prisoner, but he had never liked the uncomfortable, conflicting emotions the situation brought out in him. The guy could have killed Blaire. Maybe had wanted to. It would have been easy for Gus to treat him like a soccer ball.

But he didn't. Instead he sat beside Blaire, whom he'd helped to dismount and sit against a tree. For all she had claimed it was just a flesh wound, it was taking a toll on her. He was amazed at the strength and determination that had brought her this far.

"I wouldn't have minded having you on my team over there," he told her.

"That's quite a compliment," she murmured. "Thanks, Gus."

"You're remarkable."

"I'm a soldier." That seemed to be all she needed to say. From his perspective, it was quite enough.

Because of the chaotic winds aloft so near the peak of the mountain, the helicopter couldn't come very close or low. Through the trees he caught glimpses of three people sliding down ropes to the ground, and after them came a Stokes basket.

Then another wait.

"I wish I could go to the hospital with you," Gus said. "But the horses…"

"I know. Take care of the horses. They were good comrades today, weren't they?" She smiled wanly. "Gus?"

"Yeah?"

"I think I was running on adrenaline."

That didn't surprise him at all, but before he could respond, three men burst out of the trees in tan overalls. He instantly recognized Seth Hardin, a retired Navy SEAL who'd helped build the local rescue operations into a finely honed operation.

They shook hands briefly as the other two put Blaire on the basket and strapped her in. Gus repeated her injuries to the two EMTs, then watched them race back through the woods to get Blaire onto the helicopter.

Seth remained with him. "I'll keep watch over the prisoner if you want to head back."

Gus nodded. "I need to take care of two horses. But FYI, I didn't touch the guy's weapon or much of anything except to put the zip ties on him."

Seth arched a brow. "That must have required some restraint."

"Exactly." They shared a look of understanding, then Gus rose. "You armed?"

Seth patted his side, pointing out the rather obvious pistol attached to his belt. "Of course."

"You want one of our shotguns? He said he's alone but…"

"Hey, you know what we're capable of. I'll be fine. I'm just going to make sure this creep can't move an inch, then I'll stand back and pay attention. It won't be for long. The second chopper is supposed to be following with some more cops. You just get out of here. You don't need to wear a neon sign to tell me how worried you are about Blaire."

JEFF WALSTON WANTED to spill his guts. He started talking in the helicopter and by the time Gus was able to reach town, they had a pretty clear picture of the so-called Hunt Club.

It was an ugly one. Micah Parish filled him in as Gus drove to the hospital. Gus listened with only one ear. He could get the nitty-gritty later, but right now he was badly worried about Blaire. Blood on the outside of the body didn't necessarily mean there wasn't internal bleeding. She'd held on, probably longer than she would have without a flood of adrenaline coursing through her, but now the question was how much damage had she worsened with her stubbornness.

At the hospital they wouldn't tell him much except that she was now in recovery. He could see her when she woke up.

The wait was endless. His pacing could have worn a path in the waiting room floor. Still, pieces began to fall together in his mind. He began to see exactly where he wanted to go.

It kind of shocked him, but as it settled in, he knew it was right.

BEFORE BLAIRE EVEN opened her eyes she knew where she was. She'd been in the hospital before, and the odors plus the steady beeping of equipment placed her firmly in her present location.

As she surfaced slowly from the drugs, memory returned. Being shot, the insane ride through the woods that she would have been smarter not to do, helping Gus capture the bad guy. The ride in the Stokes basket up to the helicopter. Then nothing.

She moved a little and felt that her wound had changed. Probably surgery, she thought groggily. Yeah, her throat felt raw, so there'd been a breathing tube.

It was over. She'd be fine. She didn't need a doctor to tell her that. She'd been in worse condition once before from a roadside incendiary device. That time she'd been saved by luck as much as anything, being on the far side of the vehicle.

"Blaire."

A quiet voice. Gus. He was here. Warmth suffused her, and a contradictory sense of happiness. Lying post-op in a hospital bed seemed like an odd place to feel that warmth.

At last the anesthesia wore off enough that she could open her eyes. They lighted instantly on Gus, who was sitting beside her bed.

"Blaire," he said again, and smiled. A wide, genuine smile that communicated more than words. She was okay and he was happy and relieved about it. Then she sensed him gently taking her hand.

"Welcome back," he said. "You're fine."

"What was that all about?" she asked, her voice thick. "The guy. What was he doing?"

He told her about The Hunt Club, about how the man they had captured had been forced into committing two murders by threats against his life.

"Sport?" That almost made her mind whirl. "They were doing this for sport?"

"Two of them, evidently. They've been rounded up. The full truth will come out with time, but right now the man we caught seems eager to talk."

"Good." Then she slipped away again, still under the influence of surgical medications.

She had no sense of how much time had passed, but when she came to again, her shoulder throbbed like mad. "Damn," she said.

"Blaire?" Gus's voice again. "What's wrong?"

"My shoulder hurts worse than when I was shot."

"I'm not surprised. No adrenaline now, plus I guess they had to do some work inside you. One of the docs said you were lucky your lung didn't collapse."

Those words woke her up completely. "What?"

"You were bleeding internally. Next time you want to ride a horse when you've been shot, please reconsider." Then he pressed a tube into her hand. "Top button. Call the nurse for some painkiller."

She certainly needed some. She pressed the button and a voice came over the speaker over her head. "Nurse's station."

"Something for pain, please."

"Be there shortly."

Then she dropped the tube and her fingers reached for Gus. He replied by clasping her hand.

"Listen," he said. "You were tough. You *are* tough, as tough as anyone I've known."

Something important was coming. She could sense it. All of a sudden she didn't want that nurse to hurry. She wanted to listen to him.

"I know we've avoided this," Gus continued. "But I refuse to avoid it any longer. Nearly losing you… Well, it kind of yanked me out of stasis."

"You, too?"

He nodded. "We don't have long. I'm sure you're about to get knocked out again. But tuck this away for when you're feeling better because I don't want to take advantage of you."

"How could you?" She thought she heard the nurse's rubbery steps in the hall. Her heart began to accelerate. "Gus?"

"I love you," he said simply. "And if you don't mind, I'd like to marry you. But don't answer now. Just put it away until you're back on your feet. I promise not to pressure you. I just needed you to know."

Just as the nurse wearing blue scrubs appeared in the doorway, she felt her heart take flight. "Pressure away," she said. Then the needle went into the IV port. "I love you, too," she said before she vanished into the haze again.

A MONTH LATER, they stood before Judge Wyatt Carter and took their vows. They'd agreed to keep their jobs, to feel out their path into the future.

And they'd promised each other they were going to attend the trials of The Hunt Club. A game? Just a game had cost five lives? It was an appalling idea. It appalled Blaire even more to recognize Jeff Walston and remember they'd served briefly together. A man known to her!

But that faded as they stepped out of the court-house into a sunny August morning. The bride wore a street-length white dress and the groom wore his best Forest Service uniform.

A surprising number of people awaited them outside and began to clap. Turning to each other, they kissed, drawing more applause.

They had friends and had found love and a new way of life.

"Upward," he murmured. "Always. I love you."

* * * * *

Get 4 FREE REWARDS!

We'll send you 2 FREE Books
plus 2 FREE Mystery Gifts.

Harlequin Presents® books feature a sensational and sophisticated world of international romance where sinfully tempting heroes ignite passion.

FREE
Value Over
$20

Get 4 FREE REWARDS!

We'll send you 2 FREE Books plus 2 FREE Mystery Gifts.

FREE
Value Over
$20

Both the **Romance** and **Suspense** collections feature compelling novels
written by many of today's best-selling authors.